Carol Ann Cole

Paradise d'Entremont
Private Investigator

Book Four in the *Paradise* series

D1628810

Cover image: Meleena Amirault
Cover design: Rebekah Wetmore
Editor: Andrew Wetmore

ISBN: 978-1-990187-28-5
First edition May, 2022

2475 Perotte Road
Annapolis County, NS
B0S 1A0

moosehousepress.com
info@moosehousepress.com

We live and work in Mi'kma'ki, the ancestral and unceded territory of the Mi'kmaw people. This territory is covered by the "Treaties of Peace and Friendship" which Mi'kmaw and Wolastoqiyik (Maliseet) people first signed with the British Crown in 1725. The treaties did not deal with surrender of lands and resources but in fact recognized Mi'kmaq and Wolastoqiyik (Maliseet) title and established the rules for what was to be an ongoing relationship between nations. We are all Treaty people.

Also by Carol Ann Cole

The *Paradise* Series

Paradise
Paradise 548
Paradise on the Morrow*

Other fiction

Less Than Innocent* – co-author with more than twenty other writers. Coming in 2022.

Non-fiction

Comfort Heart—a Personal Memoir (with Anjali Kapoor)
Lessons Learned Upside the Head
If I Knew Then What I Know Now
From the Heart (with Deanna Jones)
The Cole Connection* (coming in 2022)

*from Moose House Publications

For my sisters...

Lois Young, Lorraine Rosenal and Connie Dea

Contents

Prologue

"Remember this beautiful dress, sweetheart?"

Paradise and Hope were sifting through what seemed to be a million photos, hoping to put at least half aside for the garbage. They seemed to have a duplicate of every picture taken and many were so out-of-focus it was difficult to determine who was in the frame. "No one needs this many pictures so let's do this," Paradise had said. She knew her daughter was not happy to be 'stuck' working on this project.

"It's your project, not mine, mother."

"Call it whatever you want, Hope, but I really would like to have you working through this with me. Is that so bad?"

"No. So, show me that picture you were asking if I remembered. I know you seem to remember every single picture, mom, but I'm not interested so therefore I don't remember." Hope reached for the photo her mother had been holding to her chest as they bantered back and forth.

The girls were sitting cross-legged on the living room floor with an antique suitcase holding all of the family pictures between them. Paradise made sure she passed the photo face down when she put it in her girl's hands. "Tell me what your immediate thoughts are when you turn it over and look at your younger self. What were you thinking at that very moment?"

Hope sat, mouth open, tearing up and looking almost lovingly at the photo. "Oh. My. God. Mom, you were so mad at me that day. I remember I made the decision to wear my fancy new dress to Mavillette beach while you were working. That's also the day you explained what consequences were all about. Oh yes, I remember the 'decisions we make and the resulting consequences' talk very well. For the record, I knew you were right before you even began your speech. I remember thinking for a second that you might put slides up on the wall and walk me through it."

"It didn't occur to me that your first memory would be how angry I was with you for wearing this dress to roam around the beach." Pointing to the photo, Paradise said, "I purchased that party dress for you in Toronto while we were visiting with my family—and now yours. Remember how Nana and I argued about who would pay for the dress?"

"No. I guess I zoned out when it was time to pay, but I sure was stoked to have it. I can actually remember a feeling that came over me when I walked out of the changing room to show you how pretty the dress was and you turned me around so I could see myself in a really big mirror. I decided that the blue in my dress was as blue as the ocean is on some days and the uneven hemline of my dress, which I had never seen before in my entire life by the way, reminded me how rough the ocean could be...and I loved the skinny straps because they looked a little bit like something a grownup might wear."

"I know you were 'stoked', dear, and I wanted this to be a mother and daughter memory so it was important to me that you have the dress in your closet. You weren't supposed to wear it to the beach and, for certain, you were not to wade out into the ocean while wearing it. You had, and still have, by the way, a habit of 'just going to dip your toes in' followed by a dive into a big wave coming your way because the wave was 'calling to you'. I believe that is how you explained your sand-filled and soaked dress that day, yes?"

"Okay, okay, mom. Yes, that's exactly how the day developed. You haven't commented on my Cyndi Lauper look that I created by adding my red rubber boots to complete my outfit. I almost lost those boots with the last wave that took me under."

Mother and daughter shared a laugh and gained one additional memory.

"Hope, I think it's time I purchased another beautiful dress for you. What do you think?"

"If I had somewhere special to go I would love to have a new dress...a gown! Are we going shopping even without a good reason, mom?"

"You're becoming quite the artist, Hope. I've noticed some of the drawings you have in your room. How would you feel about designing a couple of dresses for us?"

"You mean like mother and daughter dresses? Aren't we a bit old for matchy-matchy? So we're not going shopping? What is going on here, mother? And you do know I can't make a dress, right? Sure, I can draw one, but I can't actually make it."

Paradise could see Hope would require more information. She was enjoying the moment. "My darling daughter, I'm searching for the perfect way to ask you to stand beside me as Thomas and I are married. Lee will stand up (and stand still, I hope) with his father. I was trying to tell you without telling you, but clearly my clues were clueless, as you would say."

Hope wiped at the full-on stream of tears falling from her face. "Oh, mom, I will be so honoured to stand with you during your wedding. But I know one thing and one thing only about being in this position...that is you would turn and pass your flowers to me before you and Thomas do the deed. Correct?"

"I wouldn't personally call the marriage ceremony 'doing the deed', Hope but now I'm sure those words will be in my head when I pass my flowers to you. Maybe I won't look directly at you."

"So you can do the deed, mother. I rest my case."

Laughter is contagious and this was a cause for much laughter.

"I'll design a few dresses; your dress will be just a little bit formal because this marriage deserves a bit of 'formal', I think, and my dress will be the most awesome dress ever designed for a Cape St Mary teenager!"

"Thank you so much, my girl. This will be a wonderful day for the four of us and our family and friends."

Paradise had more to say, but so did her daughter. Hope was definitely engaged and clearly one picture had started the entire conversation.

"Mom, maybe you could find a way for Pops to be part of your wedding? He would be so pumped."

"I already have that covered. I haven't asked him yet, so please don't mention it, but I hope Pops will walk me down the aisle. Do you think he would like to do that for me and be part of our ceremony, or would he rather sit with Eugenie and watch it all happen? He might feel too anxious to do anything but attend. I'd be okay with that as well. I'll speak with him soon."

"Church wedding?"

"No, we will have a Mavillette beach wedding, weather permitting. If we can't be on the beach we will all fit nicely into 548 Cape St Mary Road, which is where we will all go for an informal reception after we are married."

"So, a party will happen. Can I invite some of my friends from school? To the party, I mean? Not a lot of friends, I promise."

"Make a list and we will see, Hope. We really do want everyone in attendance to be part of our lives. We'll even invite your grand-parents in Toronto. I do want you to feel that you are very much a key part of this day, so I would like you to have some friends by your side when I can't be."

"When you say, 'this day', does that mean you have already picked a date?"

Hope became part of this wedding preparation rather easily, Paradise thought. "Not yet, dear. Let me know if you have any suggestions, including dates to avoid."

"Mom, I think this blue dress is a mini version of the dress I would like to wear. Especially how the different parts of the hem-line are uneven. Your dress will be far more formal than mine."

Memories are made of this.

1: Rip-roaring mad

In Cape St Mary, life went on. The whispering continued.

"Thomas, I simply cannot believe what I'm hearing," Pops said. "Several months have passed and this nonsense never stops." Pops had grown fond of Thomas and this was breaking his heart.

Eugenie had heard it all too. "Pops, you listen to me. You get up there on that soapbox of yours and shut this gossip down."

Eugenie couldn't believe those who lived in *her* tiny village could treat such a kind man so poorly. No one deserved this.

The majority of those who attended the welcome home party for Thomas, Paradise and their children were happy to repeat the proposal that Thomas had made on bended knee. This became the number one item of gossip in the Cape. The poor man's proposal had shut the party down.

"Will you marry me?" The locals used the proposal, or a version of one, as a way to begin or end a conversation, during a meeting or even during their morning stop at Café Central. It had caught-on from day one and while some were less than comfortable being part of the local gossip-crowd they went along with the joke at the expense of a man some were beginning to love.

Conversation paused whenever Paradise or Thomas entered the Café. When they weren't there, jokes could be heard as each table emptied and people rushed off to start their day.

"Time for me to get to work. Marry me?"

"Okay I'm outa here. Will you marry me?"

"See you at the house. Will you?"

"Thanks for coffee. Should you, would you?"

"I'll pick up supper for a change so no need to cook dear. WUMM?"

The proposal that came straight from the heart had been reduced to slang.

Pops had gotten into the routine of having morning coffee at home with his bride or making the short walk over to his former home for a cup of coffee with his favourite family of four. But today was different and he was ready. Sitting at the back of the Café, at the lone table in the corner normally meant for staff, he could not believe what he was hearing. It didn't take much for him to get to his feet and block the exit.

Intentionally using his booming voice, Pops knew *everyone* could hear him. "Is this what we've become? We poke fun at someone else's heartache?"

Two men, who were about to leave, returned to their table with their heads downcast. They were afraid to walk out, thinking Pops might snag them with those huge hands of his and slap them back down.

"I'd like to WUMM everyone of ya' with my bare hands. If it's a dust-up you're after just follow me out of the Cafe when I leave." Pops looked around at each table and pointed a finger at those who seemed to think this was still a joke, "Imagine if you men, any damn one of ya', proposed to your lady in public and she said nothing. She didn't say 'no' but the silence was as bad. I wonder how that would make you feel." Pops owned a glare that held everyone hostage.

"I've been quietly sitting and listening to all of you, the whole damn lot of you. If you didn't speak up, yet you laughed. To my mind, that's just as bad. You're laughing at a man who dared to put it all out there because *he thought* everyone who gathered in his home had his back. Do you understand how many people you are letting down with this nonsense? What kind of example are you setting for Hope and all the other young 'Hopes' out there? In the name of God, I'm begging you to think this through. Cape St Mary is better than this and you know it. *You are better than this!*" Draining the last of his coffee, Pops stared at the bottom of his mug as he gathered his final thoughts. "And I'm ashamed to say, you *always* make sure the joke is on Thomas. Tell me this...does it feel good to kick a man when he's down, because it sure doesn't feel good to me. I'm disappointed in the lot of you."

Pops put his cap on and left the Café. He didn't want to hear anyone answer his question or even speak to him. He was proud and some glad he had been able to do this. He couldn't wait to share his speech with Thomas and Paradise.

After Thomas had poured his heart out to Pops, and asked for his help, Thomas knew he had gone to the right person. Pops had been quick with his response. "You leave this to me, son. I'll be the first customer at the Café tomorrow morning and after I've said my piece the gossip will stop. You mark my words!" Pops had given Thomas a big bear hug and turned to hide his tears.

"Job done!" Pops roared as he stood proudly on the stoop at the side of the Café.

~

In the privacy of their home, Thomas and Paradise had come to an understanding regarding his proposal. Paradise was desperate to make this right for Thomas. So they agreed she would do the asking. Paradise would ask Thomas to marry her when she was ready and he would keep the ring in a safe place until that day arrived.

No timeline.

No pressure.

No proposal.

No marriage.

Hope was getting organized to return to school and Lee flourished in his new home and his new surroundings. He loved the ocean. Warm or cold, windy or calm, high tide or low tide, none of the details mattered to Lee. If he was awake he wanted to go to the ocean. And he wanted to be *in* the ocean, so the family rule was, 'all eyes on the kid all the time.' Family motto.

Hope had called it 'Marvellous beach' and now Lee named it 'Marble beach.' Close enough.

Pops and his bride dropped in almost every day. Paradise loved having them over for coffee early in the morning, and they were happy to oblige. They got to enjoy a bit of quiet time with Paradise and Thomas before young Lee made his appearance for the day. To the pleasure of everyone, both Hope and Lee slept late almost every morning.

Two weeks after they settled into their new home, they concluded that nobody was in the bedroom best suited for them. So, on the morrow, everyone changed rooms. Paradise and Thomas wanted the first floor bedroom and the space to construct two small office areas they could use once the kids were in bed. Upstairs, Hope took the large bedroom and Lee the freshly-painted smaller room. He wanted his room to be 'blue like Marble beach' and even helped with the painting.

He loved his room almost as much as he loved the ocean. In fact, Lee loved everything and his parents tried to keep it that way. He was happy and always eager to make others smile with him.

Just after arriving in Cape St Mary, Thomas received a message to call Doctor Legault at the hospital in Honolulu where Wikolia had died. Thomas had tried to return the Doctor's call but so far they had not connected. He assumed the call was more of a mental check-in. The last thing Doctor Legault had said to Thomas as they shook hands was, "I'll be checking up on you, so you can expect my call."

"Understood, and I look forward to that call," Thomas had replied.

The doctor had mentioned that, in his professional opinion, Thomas had not taken time to grieve Wikolia's passing. While Thomas respected Doctor Legault, he was certain his mental health was just fine, thank-you-very-much.

2: Lusting after her

Paradise was back at work with the local police force. Sergeant Curtis had briefed her on day one of her return that the Chief Medical Examiner in Halifax had called for her...more than once. "Is there something you're not telling me, Paradise?"

Smiling, she let the question hang in the air for a bit before replying. Paradise wanted to return the call from her home for privacy reasons. "Thanks for hanging on to Doctor Scott's message for me, Curtis. Much appreciated. *If and when* there's anything to tell, you'll be the first to know. After I share with Thomas, of course."

Midway out of the office, Paradise stopped and turned to face Curtis again. Clearly she had more to say. Curtis worried that she may have witnessed him 'lusting' after her as she sashayed away on her high-heeled shoes.

"Was there something else, Paradise?" He could always hope...

Following a prolonged pause Paradise spoke. "No, I'm embarrassed. I seem to have lost my train of thought."

She walked back into the office and sat down, as if that would bring her some clarity of thought. "Oh, I remember. Forgive me for that lapse in memory, boss."

Little did she know Curtis was embarrassed for his own reasons. "What is it, Paradise? Spit it out."

"I know you'll remember I did meet with Doctor Scott when I went to the city to challenge the autopsy findings for 'Morning Glory.' I'm using her stage name to make it easier for you to recall the case."

Paradise paused as if she was finished, again, then seemed to have something else to discuss. "When I get caught up with all I have missed while in Honolulu helping Thomas pack up and then return here with Hope and me, could we pull and review the file dating back to my first bit of work with you when Morning Glory and Dawn came to town? If you're curious, pull the file, Curtis, and review how our case involving the two young ladies was closed and the comments made. Pay particular attention to the comments."

"Paradise, stop talking in riddles. I don't have time for it. I'm in charge of every case that comes through those doors. I can't afford to waste any of my time reviewing an old case to see what we may or may not have missed. Be more specific or get out of my office." He was attempting to be both angry and hurt.

Paradise wasn't sure if her boss was being serious and she wasn't impressed. She didn't have to wait long before he chimed in one more time.

Curtis was bluffing...he didn't want this conversation to end. "Why don't you pull the file right now, pick up a couple coffees and come back, and we'll get comfortable. Go out to get our coffee, though, because the stuff here at the station isn't fit to drink."

Paradise wondered when Curtis made himself the official Pooh-Bah of the Cape. "Sorry, boss, I have a couple of cases the boys have asked me to take a look at to see if I can catch something they didn't. The cases are somewhat time sensitive so I need to review and study both tonight."

Paradise was back on her feet and this time she backed up while talking until she was at his door and then she bolted. Or did she? Curtis hoped he was just being paranoid.

3: Fight night

Not a day passed that Denis and his brother, Waine Lee, didn't think of their sister. They agreed to travel to Honolulu to visit Wikolia and meet her son. Yet, something always prevented the trip from happening.

"Hey, brother, we've got a letter here from the Honolulu Fight Club." Denis threw it on the coffee table along with today's bills. Not much was getting paid and now the overdue bills were arriving.

"I'm guessing if they're looking for you and me it means a Fight Night is coming up. We should tell them we want an increase in our take of the house purse." Waine sat slumped in his favourite chair, looking not-at-all like a prizefighter.

"Not a bad idea since we win it all every time we show up. They won't admit it but the house is only full when we're in the ring." Denis was on a roll. "We've talked about this before, but we never seem to act on it. Another question for both of us is, why have we never found our own personal sponsors. We surely both know people or companies that would endorse us. We need to get moving...plus we need to get training, and this might give us the kick in the ass we need."

"Enough with the nattering and patting ourselves on the back, will you *please* read the letter." Waine was losing his patience.

"You're right. Where is it, among all these bills? What the hell has happened to our collective desire to make something of our ives?" Denis knew there was enough blame for both of them.

"*Read the damn letter,*" Waine said, in an all-too-loud voice.

Denis found the envelope addressed to both of them. He ripped open and read silently for a minute or two. "It's not what we thought, Waine. It's not really about Fight Night." Lowering his voice Denis continued, "It's about our sister. Someone is looking for her family—for us. Seems she—"

Waine cut in, "In God's name, Denis, will you *please* read the letter?"

"Well, maybe it's a bit about locating you and me, but the bottom line is, it's about Wikolia. Listen to this."

> *Dear Denis and Waine,*
> *I have some disturbing news for you.*
> *The guy Wikolia has been in love with forever has been nosing around trying to find your family. 'Any member of your family' is what he told our office girl the other day. She relayed the message to me, saying Thomas Adams seemed desperate to find Wikolia's mother in particular. He wouldn't tell us why it was such an emergency, but he kept repeating that he needed to find someone as soon as possible. More than a few weeks have passed and I'm sorry we haven't contacted you until now. I thought someone had given you a call right away but apparently not.*
> *I'm thinking you boys will be in town for our quarterly Fight Night and, of course, I'm hoping you will both participate in our private after hours 'Cage' performance. As per our house rules, last man standing will receive a nice purse for winning the main event. We have a few new sponsors for the Night and the prize money is big. I can't write much more about the event and I think you know why.*
> *Details will be sent to you in the usual manner. I assume your mailing address has not changed.*
> *Keep your training up, men, and I'll see you in the city. I'll help you find Wikolia, too. I promise.*
> *But first, we fight.*
> *Until then,*
> *The Claw*

Denis spoke first as he paced heavily on the well-worn carpet i their cluttered living room. "Those bastards. They start and end this letter with the possible disappearance of Wikolia but the middle is all about making money. It's about *us* making money for them and that's really why they're contacting us." He waved the letter around as if it was on fire but he couldn't put it down.

"When this letter says 'first we fight', they mean first you and I fight. Apparently finding our sister doesn't happen until after we perform. We'll see about that." Waine wanted to make them pay for even suggesting the brother's focus would be on fighting when their sister might be in trouble.

High fives as the Lee brothers jumped into action. 'Action' being a long jog to their local fitness club, followed by two hours of training, followed by a hot tub, followed by a long jog home.

"How did that feel, bro?" Waine finally had enough energy to breathe and speak at the same time. "Let's not stop training cold-turkey ever again. We are gluttons for punishment if nothing else."

"I feel sore, tired and excellent all at the same time," Denis said. "Why do we do this to our bodies?" Saying this he grabbed what could only be called belly fat but he did it with a smirk on his face so Waine just laughed at him.

The boys were back in training!

Wikolia didn't come first after all. They didn't mention her even once during the rest of the day. It was all about Fight Night. Waine and Denis did what they do best. They put together a training program that would prepare them to step back into the ring. Every waking hour was about training.

'The Claw' would be proud.

4: Instantly on high alert

Paradise was prepared. "It's now or never," she whispered to no one as she watched Thomas walk up Cape St Mary road to their home.

"Hi honey, I was hoping to catch you before Hope returns from school, and here you are. Do you have time to sit and talk?"

"Paradise, of course I have time to talk. I always have time for you and you know that. You seem nervous, my love, is everything okay?"

When she didn't reply, Thomas wondered if this was about Lee. "I didn't hear any noise when I came in so I'm assuming Lee is down for his nap. I hope he didn't give you a rough time this morning. He is wound up a bit more than normal these days, it seems, and I'm extra aware of that when I leave him with you."

Feeling a bit defensive, Paradise replied quickly and with her own questions in rapid fire. "Why would you say that? Have I complained about Lee giving me a rough time? What am I doing that makes you think I'm nervous? Are you trying to upset me?"

Paradise knew she was overreacting but she couldn't seem to get out of her own way. This was not going well. Too late.

"You seem to be on edge. That's all. What is it and how can I fix it for you?" Thomas hoped Paradise wasn't ill.

"I need to talk with you about something and I know you won't like it."

Thomas was losing patience. "What won't I like?"

"Lenny," came the reply. "It's about Lenny."

"He's not here I hope?" Thomas was instantly on high alert.

Paradise responded by shaking her head as she whispered, "No, of course he's not here."

"What is it then, Paradise?" Just hearing Lenny's name made his blood boil. "What is it about this man *now?*"

"Please stay calm, Thomas. I need you to hear me. Really hear me. Can you do that for me?"

Trying to lighten the mood, Thomas replied, "Sure."

"In Hawaii, when Lieutenant Commander Jalen Lexis advised us that Lenny was not on shift as we arrived to say goodbye to everyone, somehow that bit of information didn't seem to be news to you. I remember you thanking Jalen and then sharing a laugh with him. And, before you interrupt, I am not making something out of nothing. I was stunned that Jalen would make that decision on his own, which is why I asked you whether you were aware. I'm sure you remember me asking you as soon as we got into the car."

"Paradise, I don't remember it being a long discussion and I'm not sure I realized you were even upset at the time. As we were driving away from 2.0, I remember you asked if I had known in advance that Lenny would be 'locked up', and I said I had *not* known. Did I miss something?"

"Talk to me, Paradise," he added, moving to sit beside her on the window seat. "Why on earth are you bringing up Lenny, as you like to call him, when we left all that behind us a few months ago? Or, maybe I just *thought* we left it behind. I'm guessing hard-bitten Lenny is still on your mind. Am I wrong?"

Thomas knew he was shouting at Paradise, and he knew better, but just hearing news about Len, *anything about Len*, brought out the worst in Thomas. He finally stopped talking.

After a few minutes of reflection, Paradise was on her feet heading to the door, and in tears. "Please, don't follow me Thomas. A Mavillette beach walk always clears my head. I need to be alone. And, by the way, don't you ever yell at me like that again."

Trying to be a bit light-hearted she glanced back at Thomas, to give him the smallest of smiles. He did not smile back.

Before coming home to the brouhaha with Paradise, Thomas had met with Sergeant Curtis regarding a case he was consulting on. His plan was to retrieve some files from his home office before calling his business partners in Port Hope, Ontario about the case.

He, too, had news to share, but the news from Paradise blindsided him and trumped his.

Watching Paradise walk towards the beach Thomas decided he could use a good phone conversation with his partners.

"Hey, it's good to hear your voice, Thomas." Jim answered the phone in Private Investigators Unstructured (PIU) Canadian offices. "We've been wanting to reach out to you but we keep missing you."

"Do you need me for something?" Thomas said.

"Yes, we do need you for something, but first of all, we hope everything is okay with you and yours, and we hope everyone is settling in at the Cape"

"We are working out lots of kinks here but I'm hopeful for our future. So, what do you need?"

Jim wanted to ask Thomas a few more questions about their trip to Toronto and then on to Nova Scotia, but Thomas seemed a bit agitated so he continued, "The coroner's office of the Hawaii Mental Health hospital has been calling here trying to reach you on a personal and time-sensitive matter. That's how they put it when I asked if I could take a message."

Jim stopped mid-thought in case Thomas wanted to chime in. Silence. "It sounded urgent. I took the most recent call. The coroner asked if I thought I could reach you immediately and have you call him in his office at the hospital. That was a few days ago I'm afraid."

Assuming the call was regarding more paperwork following Wikolia's death, Thomas wrote down the name and number he was to call. He had wanted to talk with Paradise before making the call but, unfortunately, *Lenny* had been the only topic of conversation from the second he entered their home.

Thomas shoved the note into his pocket and would make the call another day. He was certain it wasn't as urgent as the message had stated.

Thomas and Lee had a routine. Every day, following Lee's early afternoon nap, Thomas would take his son for a walk on the beach. Lee always bounced down the stairs with a big smile on his well-rested face, eager to get to Marble beach.

Lee loved running into his family when he walked, or ran, on the beach. He was at an innocent age where he was surprised to see someone he recognized and in particular he loved running into, 'mommy.' Thomas hoped seeing Paradise might ease the strain between Lee's parents, at least for today.

The beach was always her in-full-view hideaway and Thomas knew Paradise had needed Mavillette beach today...especially given the things he had said to her as his voice became louder and louder with every word.

Definitely not my finest hour, he thought.

5: *Life* magazine circa 1946

Denis sat, with his mother's ancient copy of *Life* magazine on the table directly in front of him. Both men knew what this particular magazine had meant to their mother and they wanted to pass it on to Wikolia. The magazine was dated April 15, 1946 and, at that time, the cost was 12 cents. Their father had given this particular copy of *Life* to their mother as a wedding and birthday gift.

"Leave it to dad to spend a miserable 12 cents on mom." The brothers had nothing good to say about their father.

"This magazine is the size of a small piece of wallpaper. I know there are 136 pages in it. Isn't that a book rather than a magazine?" Denis continued even with the ache in his jaw. "I can't see the page numbers because both of my eyes are still swollen shut but I remember counting the pages when I was small, with mom watching over me. She was always watching and teaching us things if my memory is still working. In fact, even my brain hurts today. Hey, is this what they call a lamebrain, Waine?"

Denis loved his own humour and with his last comment he attempted to gently lie back, resting his head on a not-so-soft cushion. Then he laughed again.

"What are you going on and on about?" Waine was laughing at his brother's expense. He could almost see how badly Denis was hurting, but he couldn't see much either. "We didn't mail this to Wikolia because of the bloody size of it. I will admit it got a bit tattered in the mix with our boxing gloves and our fancy ring-costumes."

Waine paused to hand his brother another ice pack for his face. Over the years it had fallen to Waine to look after himself *and* Denis after a trip to Fight Night. "I'm not done talking about us and our performance in that bloody ring, After all, it's not every day we receive an invitation from the Fight Club resulting in us winning every match. And one more time, we ended up in the Cage facing each other for the main event. Biggest purse we've seen so far and it all belongs to you and me, brother. Sorry you didn't claim the title of *last man standing*, Denis. Actually I'm not sorry about that at all. It was you or me."

"Yes, well 'winner take all' doesn't sound all that fair when you win every match over a three day period only to lose the Cage match." Denis wasn't happy. "Second place pays nothing? Not a damn cent."

"I hate to remind you, but what do we call second place?" Waine continued to enjoy this. Too much, perhaps.

"Loser."

"Brother, we might need to tack a few more days on to this trip. We can't go looking for our sister with these faces. I'm no better looking at the moment than you, in case you're wondering. I do have one good eye and between us that's not a good thing."

"I really feel it's time we meet her kid. I know Wikolia *says* he belongs to Thomas. Do you believe that's true, or does she just *want* it to be true?"

Denis seemed deep in thought as he mentioned Thomas Junior. Both uncles hated their nephew's name, but they would keep that to themselves when they sat down with Wikolia.

One thing at a time, just like their mother taught them. Waine and Denis could still hear her voice. "Boys if you can't win 'em all, tackle everything you take on in life, one thing a time and as long as you give it your all, you will make your mother happy. I want you to remember I taught you that even after I'm gone. *Do you hear me?"*

They were both made to say, "Yes, Momma," when she asked the question. Silence, or a nod, was never acceptable, even after they became adults.

Later that day, after ordered-in meals that included a full loaf of bread each, huge steaks, and maybe a bit of whisky, the Lee boys sat down to take stock of their bank account, their bodies, and their brouhaha abilities. No question, professional fighting paid the bills. However, their minds were beginning to cloud over and they both felt they were in trouble health-wise. They agreed to listen to their bodies and their minds, or at least try.

"Just between us, I don't think I have another Cage fight in me," Denis said. "I certainly can't battle you again. I think we should re-tire from the Cage with you on top. I'll even let you keep the title, which tells you how much I hurt right now."

Waine could see his brother out of his good eye and he knew he was serious.

Denis wasn't finished yet and almost seemed to nod off for a few minutes before speaking again. "I'm sitting here like an idiot, with my fingers on the cover of this magazine. I'm thinking of mom and our brawling family. She whopped our asses more than a few times, but she sure did teach us to fight."

"Do you think mom would be proud of us if she was sitting here today? Us looking like this, I mean."

"Oh, I think you know the answer to that. Mom would most likely position us face to face, and then she would level her famous head-butt using our heads and saving her own. I think we were in our 20s before we were able to stay on our feet after one of her head-butts. Remember mom telling us she did this out of love as she slammed our heads together?" Denis was by far the more emo-tional of the brothers. That would change in time.

Both men leaned back in their comfortable lounge chairs and rubbed their aching heads. Not a good day for either of the Lee boys. They decided to take a nap and pick the conversation up on the other side.

With their Fight Night winnings came a small, two-bedroom

apartment for as long as they needed it...or for as long as it took to rest their battered and beaten bodies. The apartment was in downtown Honolulu, and if ever they could see out of their swollen eyes they would go for a stroll down Kalakawa Avenue.

"We're not getting any younger," Waine shouted to his brother as he slammed his bedroom door.

Naps were becoming the norm...Waine knew they were both embarrassed about yet another bad habit.

6: Bamboozled

Following short naps, as it turned out, the brothers were back at it. Denis let Waine saunter down the hall, shuffle to the sofa and settle in before he began. "My God, Waine, we took such a beating trapped in that goddamn cage. How is it possible that we didn't know we were advertised as the main event? *We* were advertised as the main event. This doesn't make us look too smart. In fact, in a couple of pictures I saw after the event we looked a bit bamboozled, and that's on us."

"There's that lamebrain again," Waine and Denis said almost in unison. They were both feeling a bit more upbeat after their naps.

"I'll make this easy," Denis said. "I'm done. Mom didn't give us the best schooling she could afford so we could get our heads bashed in. I don't know about you, but with each fight, each blow to my poor head, I hurt more and more. I know I'm not thinking clearly and you and I talked about this after our fighting matches years ago. We've talked about this for a very long time. All we do is talk about it. No action. The list of my aches and pains gets longer with each fight. How badly would you hate me if you had to go solo from here on in?"

"Let's not roll over and die right here." Waine wasn't sure he liked where this discussion was going. He silently admitted he didn't disagree, though. He just wasn't quite ready to admit it.

"Cut the drama, Waine. That's not where I'm going with this conversation, and you know it. No one is rolling over and dying, but I do think we could get a bit smarter if we stop having our brains rearranged every time we step into the ring."

Denis took time to collect his thoughts before continuing. "Hear me out. Our sister might not even know mom's dead. I say we put all of our thoughts and our bank balance toward bringing our sister home."

With that Denis pointed to their cash winnings from the Fight Club. "And there it is, my brother. All we have in this world is right there in front of us. The plastic bag is a tad insulting, don't you think? And when they get all fancy like and present the winnings they call it a *purse*. 'The purse for tonight's Cage Fight goes to our celebrity champion and an excellent friend to the club, the dapper Mr. Denis Lee.'"

"It could be worse, bro. What would either you or I do with a purse...an actual purse?" Denis and Waine shared a long laugh.

"We needed that," Denis said, all smiles.

"It all sounds good, but we don't even know where Wikolia is or where we start to look for her. I say once we find Wikolia we talk her into moving home with us. And if she won't, then I say let's you and me open up shop here in Honolulu. Seems right we should be together, no? The three musketeers, as mom called us, all those years gone by."

"I'm all in. We need to figure out if any of our former buddies are still around. Let's only call the ones who know Wikolia so we can make sure we stay on track. I'll start with the phone book. We've been away a long time...it won't be easy."

Over the next few days the boys learned a few things. So they wouldn't forget stuff, they wrote everything down in a journal just like they remembered Wikolia doing. They grew up loving to tease their sister about her journal entries and her daily lists. Now they needed one because their brains had been rearranged and they would never be able to remember everything they had to do.

Everything they needed to know, in particular about the Fight Club, was already in their journal. They added a tab for Wikolia, so everything they would need to have with them at all times would be in the journal and on a list.

1. Thomas Adams had a phone number at one time but it had been disconnected with no forwarding phone number and no address.

Clearly Thomas wasn't still with Wikolia, and that made Denis and Waine happy. A little thing, but at least they had something to be happy about.

2. Neither Wikolia Sky Lee or Wikolia Sky was listed in a phone book or anywhere else they looked.
3. Asking around while at the Flight Club, Denis received some startling news. The desk clerk, Carman, had spoken with Thomas Adams and said he was frantic and desperate to find Wikolia's family.

"He didn't say Wikolia was dead but he came close. Something about a Mental Hospital, a pregnancy and Thomas being on the night shift. He wasn't making much sense and, to be honest, I just wanted him out of the Club. He kind of gave me the creeps."

As an afterthought Carman added, "And with all the creeps I see coming through our doors with boxing gloves over their shoulders, believe me, I know creeps."

4. Carman helped the Lee brothers find the name of the largest mental health hospital in Waikiki. They had an address and one day, when they could see themselves entering a mental hospital, they would be on their way.

They weren't keen on going any time soon. Too many bruises on their swollen faces to visit with their sister. She would probably get out of bed and deck them both.

In spite of all this, Denis and Waine promised each other that the second their faces looked a bit more normal, or at least were not black and blue, they *would* find Wikolia. They kept putting it off until tomorrow. Always tomorrow.

The last thing the brothers wrote on their list said:

5. Bruises gone. Life magazine in the car. Time to find our sister.

It might not be a full list, but it was a start.

Waine and Denis were 100% committed to finding Wikoilia. They were also frightened for what might lie ahead. If Wikolia was dead and someone had defiled their sister's memory, there would be Hell to pay!

7: Barrel of laughs

Hope was having a great discussion with her mother. They had not been getting along, so this was a nice change. It felt good to laugh.

"So, I'm *old* to just be starting my period now? I kind of get that, but will the cramps go away once my body gets used to this eventually, like tomorrow? Next week? Next month?" Hope's last comment was the beginning of the chuckle.

"Oh, honey, I wish I had good news about how long the periods and the cramps will go on, but I will just say I have the same cramps to this very day that I first had at your age. They have not weakened one bit."

"Well, aren't you a barrel of laughs, mother!"

"The truth hurts sometimes, Hope."

"Very funny. I'm not laughing."

"I will share a funny story with you, Hope, and I guarantee you will laugh even harder. My mother, not my birth mother but your Nana Rhodes, did *not* prepare me for my first period. I thought I was bleeding to death and I acted as if that were true. Mom had not even given me a hint that this would happen to me. And, to add insult to my most terrible day ever, mom gave me one of her *pads* and then sent me to the store to buy a box of my own that I would keep in my room. Hidden in my room, I might add. Imagine my shock, just walking to the corner store with this pad pinned to my undies.

"I walked into the store and added embarrassment to my out-of-control emotions when I realized the handsome guy who waited on me went to my school and I saw him all the time. Then I had to ask for a bag because he just took my money and handed me the box without even putting it in a bag. Finally, Hope, I assumed this happened to boys, not just girls. But oh, no, we have to protect the boys, as my mother explained it."

Mother and daughter were laughing so hard they were holding their sides, saying everything hurt. But this time it was coming from a good place.

8: Yes and no

Doctor Sydney Scott tried, and failed, to reach Paradise at the Cape police station. Sergeant Curtis advised that Paradise was 'out of town' but he would give her Doctor Scott's message as soon as possible.

There was no return call, and enough time had passed. If Paradise wouldn't return her call at work she might answer her home phone.

Not terribly professional of me, she thought, but the phone was already ringing so too late to change the plan now.

"Hello?" came a shrill and seemingly out-of-breath voice.

"Yes, hello, is Paradise there and may I speak with her, please?"

"Yes and no, to answer your two questions."

That was rather rude, thought Doctor Scott.

The voice on the other end of the phone wasn't finished. "So help me God, if this is you, Francis with-an-i, you need to know both of my parents are at my school this morning speaking with the principal so you better stop calling me right now before—"

"I am not Frances with one eye, or whatever you just said, young lady. This is Sydney Scott, Doctor Scott, Chief Medical Examiner for Nova Scotia, and I'm calling from Halifax to speak with Paradise. I still do not know whom I'm speaking with so you have me at a disadvantage. I'll go out on a limb though. Is it Paradise's daughter, Hope? Is that you? I hope to meet you in person one day."

"Is my mother sick? What does a Chief Medical Examiner do when a patient comes to see you, anyway? I'm always the last to know anything in this house, but if mom is sick, don't I have a right to know?"

"Hope, please *listen* to me. Your mother is *not* sick. I examine bodies of those who have passed away, so you have nothing to worry about. You can call me Sydney, by the way. I believe your mom calls me by my first name so you can do the same."

"I'm sorry, but I still don't know why you're calling mom because for sure she is not dead. Paradise is who you want, right? Oh. My. God. I know I'm asking too many questions, but do you mean 'passed away' as in *dead?*"

"I believe I asked for Paradise when you answered the phone, Hope. I don't know about your schedule for today, but I have several dead bodies waiting for me to work on them."

There was a small gasp at the other end of the line. "Hope, that was unprofessional of me and your mom will not be pleased with me for talking so openly and freely with you about the bodies calling my morgue 'home' at the moment. Can you please just give her my message?"

"Sure," came the one word answer followed by a dial tone. Hope had hung up on the doctor.

First time for everything thought Doctor Scott. It would be interesting to hear what Hope tells her mother. She was sure her 'dead bodies' comment would find its way to Paradise, and that's what she wanted.

Hope now had three reasons to be anxious for her parents to return home from her school. She needed to know how they made out talking to Principal Paul and, more importantly, was Francis with-an-i at her desk when they arrived? And now this weird call.

Checking the clock on the kitchen wall Hope was surprised to see it wasn't even 10 am and things were already hopping in her world. She wrote a quick note to her parents before taking Lee for his morning strut along Mavillette beach.

For some reason, when Lee was at the beach he walked with a strut. Hope thought it might be the way he dug each foot into the sand before taking another step, but she wasn't positive about that. She made a mental note to watch his exact walk more closely and see if she could influence him to walk as he normally does. *But, what's wrong with strutting?* "Parents," she wrote on the blackboard in the kitchen, "the boy has taken me to Mavillette beach.

The time is 10:10 am. We will strut or gallivant or whatever Lee has on his mind today. Maybe you could come and find us if you aren't too busy? Mom, please see my note on your desk."

> *Mom, this story is too long for the blackboard and I want to write it down before I forget. I may not have this information totally accurate but here goes: A doctor who lives in Halifax and works on dead bodies that she keeps in her house is looking for you. She said she has been trying and trying to talk with you. Sydney...that's her name and she said I could call her that which I found a bit funny because if Sydney is her name what else would I call her? We didn't get into that though because I didn't want her to be more agitated.*
>
> *Mom, it's possible she's been looking for you since we went to Honolulu to help dad and Lee.*
>
> *So, I'm begging you, please call her so she won't call and surprise me a second time. (And I do want to know all about the dead body stuff she was talking about.)*

9: Underground thugs

Wilmot and Marie sat back with their eyes closed and enjoyed the train ride taking them 'up the line.' Wilmot was thinking about his sister, Paradise, and how fortunate he was that they lived so close to each other.

Additionally, he knew how fortunate he was that someone had found him the night Meat Cove had beaten him nearly to death. He thanked Paradise's God that he had survived. Being reunited with his family had been extremely emotional.

Finding his bride and learning the underground thugs in the belly of the gang wars in Toronto, and Meat Cove in particular, were responsible for the vicious beating Marie endured was almost impossible to hear. Wilmot knew this was his fault. He knew where Marie worked when he met her and he had done nothing about encouraging her to quit.

Marie healed slowly from her wounds, but she did heal, so she won in the end and Wilmot was terribly proud of her. She learned to walk and talk and put her words together to form sentences all over again, without complaint even though she endured many lengthy and painful surgeries to put her back together.

Marie's bi-annual checkup would be the next day and she was anxious to catch up with her medical team. They were the angels who picked her up and slowly put her back together and she would forever be grateful to them. They had believed in her when she had not. She was tired of hearing her name and the word 'con-valesce' in the same sentence and made a mental note to bring that up in a joking way with her doctor.

"Are you awake, Wilmot?"

Reaching for her hand, Wilmot replied, "I am, Marie, and clearly you are as well. Are you okay?"

"I am. The scenery along the Valley is brilliant if you want to open your eyes and see it. Let's make this trip when I don't have medical appointments to get to. Wouldn't that be a lovely way to spend a summer day? Before you say it, I realize you could drive us, but then you wouldn't be able to see what I'm seeing. Does that appeal to you at all?" "At the moment I'm more focused on tomorrow. Are you nervous about seeing your doctor, my love? I'm hoping the lull of the train is helping you relax a bit."

"I'm not nervous at all, which is a bit surprising. Putting me back together was the easy part and I know at least two of my appointments are with those who reattached everything and stitched me up. I'll never be called statuesque and, as you know my skin looks like a patchwork quilt with all the zigs and zags and many colours. Wilmot, I'm a bit proud of my scars, though. It sounds a bit silly but I feel like a warrior princess."

"And you're *my* warrior princess. My beautiful and strong princess." Wilmot had finally opened his eyes to watch the scenery. He didn't quite see the beauty in everything passing by in a blur, however inside the train he was enjoying the beauty of his wife.

"I know it's not a competition, Marie, but I think you win the prize for the most stitches and colour patches and, of course, your positive attitude."

Smiling almost to herself Marie said, "I heard how beautiful I was for months and months from my therapist."

"Should I be jealous?" Wilmot was joking as he leaned over to kiss his warrior princess.

10: Cape royalty

Pops and Eugenie put a smile on everyone's face as they watched Cape St Mary's favourite bride and groom stroll along the beach, hand in hand. On the days when Eugenie's knees were not cooperating she held her cane in one hand and her husband's hand in the other. Memories are made of this.

Pops and Eugenie were getting more exercise once they began walking every day.

"*Every single day?*" came from Pops when Eugenie first suggested they walk and try to lose a couple pounds. They had both gained a noticeable amount of weight and they hadn't been married for all that long when their much-needed exercise routine began.

While Pops didn't feel he had gained even one pound, he was happy to go along with 'the plan' because he could see that Eugenie had indeed gained a fair amount of weight. Pops did not ask for weight-related details.

"We're not only happy, Pops. We're happy *and* we're fat. How did this happen behind our backs? Do *not* answer that if you know what's good for you. I know all too well what's behind my back!" Eugenie laughed at her own expense.

Pops cautiously said, "Love, you just tell me when to walk and where. I don't need any further details, trust me."

Initially their exercise route was anything but exercise since everyone they met wanted to stop and chat. Eugenie allowed this to happen for the first week...she was ready for this and she introduced the same line to everyone as they walked along as briskly as their legs would allow. "Walk with us if you like but we have to keep moving."

For the most part, friends and neighbours only heard the, "Walk with us..." but they understood. *Honeymooners want to be alone!*

Since their wedding, they had tried, modified and tried again to develop a daily routine. They were both in the habit of getting up and dressed very early. Any time after six am you could be guaranteed a light would go on in their home. Neither Pops nor Eugenie moved very quickly first thing in the morning so they made sure to never accept an invitation that would mean they had to leave home prior to 7:30. Ideally 8:30.

Paradise had invited Pops and Eugenie to have breakfast with her and the family at what had become known as 'the big house', any day or every day. The open invitation was a sincere one and they didn't take it for granted. They both joined the family around 8 or 8:30 as often as possible.

There were days, though, when Eugenie stayed behind, choosing to be lazy at home. Alone. Eugenie felt strongly that a bit of space from each other was good for their marriage and a few early morning hours alone were just what she needed.

Pops had no idea and this always made Eugenie smile. He would never know, and if he ever read her mind and figured it out she would think of something else to ensure they both had their alone time! Her husband was used to reacting anytime she said, 'I need...' and once she learned this she had dropped 'I' from her vocabulary. 'We need...' seemed more inclusive, she thought.

Not for the first time, while sipping her coffee in silence, Eugenie thought back to her younger days.

A native of Cape St Mary, she was shipped off to the convent when she left school in her early teens. *Not her decision!* Her first assignment while she lived 'on the inside' was to be sent outside of the convent to baby-sit or supervise children while their parents worked.

The first time Mother Superior approached Eugenie following prayer time and asked how she was managing with her first duty she didn't realize there were things she should say and things she should not say. Eugenie had explained to Mother Superior that she had told one of the dads his son was spoiled. He repaid her honesty by reporting her saying his child was *not* spoiled. She proceeded to provide unwanted examples of the kid's behaviour, which meant she was digging an even deeper hole for herself.

Mother Superior was momentarily relieved to hear Eugenie say that she had learned from this experience. Eugenie changed the words she used, but was once again reported by an angry mother who made it clear she did not feel her daughter was being coddled, as Eugenie had suggested.

Eugenie tried to recall the exact discussion that would keep her in the Mother House for most of her life. "It seems I can't win though, Mother Superior. When I explained, and gave examples of why I felt her daughter was being coddled she shot back with, 'That's like saying she's spoiled and my daughter is certainly not spoiled.' At the time, I had thrown my arms in the air, saying, 'I give up.' And, bless me Lord, or you, Mother Superior, I left my assignment mid-day vowing never to return. In fact I never did return to that assignment so either the Lord or someone on the inside took pity on me."

Having started, Eugenie had more to say. "That action meant I had about a hundred rosaries to say, if you know what I mean. I guess you do know. It's just that I want to ensure you're aware that I've already been punished for my actions."

Shortly after this discussion with Mother Superior, Eugenie was taken off the list of nuns deemed suitable for work outside of the convent.

As Eugenie sat alone, reviewing the sins of her past, she thanked God she had made the decision to finally leave the convent when she did. Returning to Cape St Mary had been daunting in so many ways. If she had to list a few examples...

> Never lived alone. (Convent excluded.)
> Never cleaned her own apartment. (Convent rooms were the size of a prison cell.)
> Never had a paying job.
> Never paid a bill.
> Never purchased anything with her money.

Never saw a man without his shirt on until that hot summer day when she watched ten men putting a new roof on a house right there on Cape St Mary road. *Shirtless. My Land.*

Never went to a coffee shop until Café Central in the Cape.

Never had a female friend she was close to until Marie.

Never had a friend 'on the outside' until Pops.

Never had a date...until Pops.

Never fell in love...until Pops.

Married to her Lord...second and final marriage to Pops!

11: Francis-with-an-i

Francis with-an-i thought the interview had gone well. Better than well, actually. She checked all the boxes concerning her work life and personal life just the way the 'big man in charge' wanted them checked.

The personal questions ticked Francis with-an-i off to the point where she almost jumped up and said something that would have ended her interview all too soon. "Are we still in the Stone Age or is it just you and your school?"

She didn't say any of those things and was proud of herself for keeping her mouth shut. *There's a first time for everything,* she thought as she patted herself on the back.

Francis with-an-I knew she would remember the list of questions forever, and the hangdog expression principal Paul tried to pull off as he asked them.

"So young lady;

Do you have a boyfriend?

Do you miss work during your 'monthly's? Always/some of the time/hardly ever/never?

When you get married will you want to have a child?

If you have more than one child, will you still come to work with two or more kids at home?

Will you agree to respect our policy of never dating a co-worker?

Will you keep up your appearance even if it means dieting?"

It was all Francis with-an-i could do to keep her cool. She would be willing to bet that they never asked men such personal questions.

Francis with-an-i was all-dolled up for her interview...she knew men like that. She had found out that the 'uniform' female teachers and staff were expected to wear included buttoning your blouse up to your neck. Wearing a jacket so that your breasts are totally covered. God, she even wore a pair of slacks that were too big for her...wouldn't want them to catch a glimpse of her tight young ass!

The only glitch in her interview that Francis-with-an-i could think of was her reaction at the mention of her name, and the possible need to 'shorten it to Francis.'

God, she hated living like this! However, at the moment she just couldn't find a way to break out of the secretarial pool and find a job worthy of her talents. *A few come to mind*, she thought, *but I'm pretty sure the pay cheque wouldn't be that great or that regular*.

She needed her pay cheque to be in her hands every second week without fail just like everyone else. What she really needed in the moment was a teaching position.

In thinking it over post-interview, she assumed she would be okay. Always walking that line between a small lie and an egregious lie, Francis-with-an-i was relatively certain they would not check her references. She had said she had personally requested her references and that she would bring them to the principal as soon as they arrived. He bought it without hesitation!

That was the egregious lie...no references would be coming her way. No *good* references, for sure.

During the interview, the principal asked her to call him 'principal Paul.' What a joke. He didn't seem all that bright, and Francis with-an-i figured she could do his job with her eyes closed. *Better not share that with anyone until I actually have the job*, she thought.

The academic world was not the world she lived in other than to earn a salary...and to meet the young ladies. Francis with-an-i knew what the principal wanted because she had been around enough of them to know all men thought they were big men. And, Lord knows, they all seem to be in charge. She was getting sick of it.

I hope to God above that this world changes some day and allows a woman to at least compete for the big jobs, and one day actually land one of them,' said no one ever, thought Francis with-an-i.

12: A few silly words

The first day of school was less than two weeks away and Paul knew what was expected of him as principal of the only high school for a number of counties. The school principal was to ensure the students were learning, the parents were supportive, the cleanliness of all inside areas of the school was maintained and the secretary was happy.

Paul made a point of sharing with every candidate for a position at his school that he would make it his business to keep his secretary happy, and that, in return she would ensure everyone else in the school was happy. A rule that may have seemed a bit unbalanced but it worked for Paul and it always drew laughter.

Francis with-an-i thought it made him seem like a wanna-be comedian. Or a clown, which was so much worse.

Francis with-an-i aced the interview and she knew it, even though Principal Paul said pompously that the successful candidates would receive a call from someone on the board. Until that time no candidate was to call the school. If Francis-with-an-i had not received a call by the weekend prior to the opening of the school in September, she could assume all positions were filled. All successful candidates would have to read, sign, have witnessed and hand in to the principal a document by the end of the first week of school. The witness could be principal Paul.

What a surprise, thought Francis-with-an-i.

"Principal Paul, everyone *will* love me, you just wait and see. And I will love them right back." She saw him lean back a little bit, like she was laying it on too thick. "Let's not jump to conclusions, Francis. Can I call you that?" he said. "Just Francis, I mean, without the *with-an-I* affix? If you hope to work in a school like ours, your name shouldn't be an issue, and I for one don't understand the meaning of, or the need for, tacking a few silly words on every single time you advise someone of your name."

Francis with-an-i opened her mouth to speak then shut it again. All the things she wanted to say collided with each other and jammed in her throat.

"Okay, I watched you bristle just now. Clearly. using a proper name presents a challenge in your eyes, so let's not discuss it right now. I'm serious about this, though, so think long and hard, young lady. If and when we bring you back for a second interview we can talk further. Sleep on it…"

Oh, if he only knew, thought Francis with-an-i.

13: Time before Cole

Elise and Paradise were having a heart to heart as they sat with their toes buried in the sand on a bright sunny day. It was a perfect Mavillette Beach day.

The stories Elise was able to share about Paradise's mother sometimes overwhelmed Paradise, but she always needed more. She felt a bond with her mother that, before meeting Elise, hadn't existed.

"Elise, I would love it if, today, you could tell me more about the young men who were in my mother's life when she started to date. I mean in the time frame before Cole arrived on the scene."

"My dear girl, that won't take very long. Cole was the only boy and the only young man, if I can call a sixteen-year-old a man, that your mother had eyes for. Madeline and Cole knew each other almost from birth. They began dating once Cole turned sixteen. Your mother, by the way, and I'm not casting judgment, *had just turned* fifteen years old, and she was still fifteen when she gave birth."

Paradise knew there would be many pauses as Elise shared her memories. She noticed that more and more often, Elise would be lost in her own thoughts and needed a moment before she could recall or continue sharing her precious memories. Paradise had learned to be patient. Some memories were painful.

"Paradise, you're always so patient with me. Thank you for that. I am telling you things, I have never in my lifetime spoken about out loud. Your mother and I talked about everything. As an example, we didn't have mother's to talk with us about having sex with boys, so we relied on each other. Madeline was the first to have sex. I didn't have a boyfriend, so she was my 'teacher', as we would often say. We were laughing, of course."

Elise paused once again and turned to make sure her young friend was smiling. She was, so Elise felt comfortable continuing. "I don't want to betray too many of her secrets but I don't think she would mind my sharing them with her daughter! Having a child was not part of their plan, but your mother and father instantly changed their plans and seemed to be totally fine with their revised list of things to do and by what date. Madeline wrote the list and Cole agreed to everything. Their only concern related to Pops. They needed his blessing and his help, and they didn't want to let him down. He had already been so good to them in many ways."

Paradise could see that Elise was hesitating again, and wanted to give her an out if she wanted to 'call it a day.' "Elise, as you know, I love these memories you are able to share with me. It's as if I am listening to my mother share her life through you. Have I tired you out for today or do you want to stay a bit longer?"

"My land, child, don't you want to know what was on their very first list of things to do?""I would love to hear every single thing that was on that list," Paradise replied as she reached out and gave her friend a hug.

"Well...first thing Cole wanted to do was find a doctor for your mother. Madeline was healthy and she did her best to convince Cole it was much too early to spend the few dollars they had saved up on medical bills before they needed to."

"I hope she didn't convince him?"

"One thing you have to know, Paradise, is that your mother had complete control of everything that involved her and Cole as a couple. Oh, she let him think he had a say in everything, but he didn't. I think he knew that. There would be no doctor unless she got sick." Elise hoped she wasn't turning Paradise against her father, but didn't want to ask. "Your mother had not even finished high school, that didn't bother her one bit. She was pretty ill with morning sickness anyhow, so she was totally consumed with that for many months. Cole was university bound and Pops was already bragging about his grandson being the first in the family to go to university. He was some nervous to tell Pops that their priorities had changed. Madeline told me she could hear his heart beating

50

beside her."

"Did my mother and father approach Pops together?"

"They approached Pops hand in hand and said they had made a few changes in their lives and hoped for his blessing. Cole would work for a while to save some money because they wanted to get an apartment, and then they wanted to get married and then they were getting a baby and this would all be completed within seven months. As I remember your mother telling me, it was at this stage of 'disclosure', as they called it, that Cole asked if he could fish with Pops. That's when Pops exploded. Madeline told me he was frozen in place as he listened to them and she didn't think Pops would be supportive at all."

Elise made a frowny face and pretended to be Pops. "'Wait a second you two. Wait just a damn second. What about all the plans you have to get an education and have a successful career and *not* be a fisherman for your entire life?' Then Pops turned to your mother. 'Madeline, was that a lie when you told me you were going to finish high school and then take that secretary's course up the line? What about that?'

"Then Cole interrupted. 'Hang on there, Pops, don't you—' 'Don't you, "don't you" me. I wasn't born yesterday. I can see the only thing in this plan of yours that comes with a timeline is a child. You're both still children but I'll say no more about that. Don't you interrupt me again, Cole. You'll know when I'm finished.'" Elise shook her head, laughing at the memory.

Paradise was intrigued to see where this story was going, but they decided to stop there. The ladies hugged loud and long and went their separate ways.

14: Dead or alive

Learning there was a possibility of Wikolia's death had rocked Denis and Waine to their core. Was this the *urgent* reason Thomas was trying to contact them?

Refusing to accept the worst-case scenario, Denis and Waine were on their way to the Mental Health Facility in Honolulu, hoping to find their sister. They had not been able to confirm Wikolia was a patient at the hospital, however, and her name was registered as a death at the hospital. This was a mistake of course, but it made finding her more urgent. They were running out of excuses and couldn't put it off any longer.

The Lee brothers were a wreck as they arrived at their destination. Sitting in their rental car in the parking lot near the biggest building they had ever seen both Denis and Waine were speechless.

"Good God, how many people in Honolulu need a Mental Health hospital?" Denis asked though he knew there would be no response. Waine hadn't said much since they called the hospital the previous evening.

"It's the second confirmation we have received that she's dead, Waine. You have to suck it up. I need you with me not just in body when we go inside. We can't sit here all day."

"What if it's true, Denis? What if Wikolia has been dead all this time and no one told us? What if she died alone?" Waine was speaking in a whisper, but at least this told Denis he understood what was happening.

"Don't get ahead of yourself. Let's go in and get some answers. We'll start with the information desk and go from there."

"Okay."

Once out of the car, Waine and Denis were content to take their time heading toward the main entrance to the hospital.

The motel clerk where the boys were staying while their faces and other body parts healed from Fight Night had told them to go inside and look for a very large 'Information' sign. She had been flirting with both Denis and Waine, and in the moment they didn't care. As long as she told them how to navigate their way to their sister, they would smile at her every damn time they came into or left the motel.

Waine was the first to spot it. "Information," was all he said as he pointed to the desk. He let Denis approach the clerk on his own because his legs wouldn't take him there.

Denis found a chair for Waine to sit in. "I need you to stay here, do you hear me? I can't keep an eye on you while I'm asking for her room number and all that. I'll be right over there at the main desk that you found for us. That was good work, bro. I'll come back here to get you, I promise."

Denis realized he was talking to Waine as he would to a young child, but it seemed to be necessary. He had never felt more alone, and he wondered if Waine was feeling the same way.

"Please, miss. *Please*. I'm begging you to check again. We know she's in this hospital somewhere. Try every combination of Wikolia Sky Lee, please. We're desperate to find our sister."

Denis wasn't sure he wanted to ask the next question but he didn't have a choice. "Miss, what about deaths?" He tried to lower his voice, so Waine wouldn't hear. He had his eyes trained on Denis and hadn't moved a muscle.

The expression changed on the Information girl's face. "Wait a minute. Show me some ID immediately or I swear to God I will have you thrown out of this hospital. If your own sister was dead, are you telling me you wouldn't know? You would come to the Information desk and ask if your sister was dead?"

Hearing the raised voice, Waine was immediately out of his chair and by his brother's side. Denis had his back to the clerk. He put his arms around his brother and, trying to keep the mood light, said, "If we're really lucky today, Waine, the security team will come and throw us out on our ass while telling us Wikolia Sky Lee did *not* die in this hospital. Wouldn't that be great?"

Silence was all Waine could offer. He was trying to speak, trying to feel more like himself, but his mind seemed to be stuck, or frozen or something. Waine needed to know what was happening to him. He had had panic attacks in the past but right now he needed to be there for his brother. But he couldn't do it.

Once they had located Wikolia, Waine was certain she would be able to help them both. She would love the *Life* magazine they had for her, too.

Only moments later, the Information clerk spoke quietly as she came out from behind her desk. "Please follow me, gentlemen. I apologize for my attitude a few moments ago. I don't know what I was thinking. Please make yourself comfortable in this room and someone will be here to speak with you momentarily. Can I get anything for you? Coffee?"

"Two black coffees would be great, miss, and thank you for your help." Denis spoke for his brother as well as himself. "I've been told I can be headstrong when necessary and I hope I haven't made you feel uncomfortable around my brother and me."

He would worry about his brother later. Clearly there was something going on in Waine's head, but Denis didn't have the schooling to deal with an emotional crisis that turns you silent.

Denis and Waine drained and crushed their coffee cups while they waited for someone, anyone, to bring them to their sister. Denis had his eyes focused on the door. Waine stared at Denis.

Time seemed to stand still, and they both seemed unaware that almost two hours had passed since the clerk had escorted them to this private room. Denis was vaguely beginning to wonder whether everyone had gone home for the day.

Finally, the door opened.

15: Focus on me

"Gentlemen, my name is Doctor Carl Legault. Please call me Carl. We have some catching up to do, but first things first. I have to ask you for identification."

Before Denis could speak, Waine was on his feet. His face was beet-red and he was yelling. "Identification? Do you know how many times we've had to pull out our ID when all we want is to see our sister?"

Putting both arms around his brother, Denis spoke in a much quieter voice. "I'm Denis and this is Waine." Turning to his brother Denis said, "Waine, look at me. Focus on me. They only asked for our identification once in this hospital. I think you're adding all the situations together where we have been asked for ID, right?"

"Sorry," Waine said. He didn't look at either the doctor or his brother.

"You have nothing to apologize for," the doctor replied.

Denis felt the doctor watching them closely, and it made him itchy. He didn't want awkward questions or even kind words. He just wanted the true truth about Wikolia. "Are you Wikolia's doctor? And when can we see her? I think my brother will snap out of whatever trance he's in once we talk with our sister. Waine's never been like this before, doctor, and I'm out of my depth here."

Doctor Legault leaned forward. "I was your sister's main doctor here at the Institute. She was with us for just over one year."

Waine interrupted, "I don't like the 'was' in what you just said, as if my sister is 'past tense'. Did Wikolia go to another hospital? You're going to give us the name and address of that place *right now* so we can get out of your hair." Denis turned and gathered his brother in his arms as he sobbed and shook. They were both frightened.

Doctor Legault said, "Wikolia suffered from extreme mental illness. I will take you through the details of her health if you like, but I need to tell you that your sister has passed away. I'm so very sorry for your loss. Please let me know what you need."Waine was on his feet again and had found his outside voice. "Do I need anything? *Anything?* What kind of a stupid question is that? Yes, I need my sister and I need her right now."

Denis pulled his brother back down into his chair and tried to hug him even tighter just to keep him from taking a swing at the doctor. He thought he had probably hugged Waine more within the last twenty-four hours than in their entire lives to date. In the moment, Denis wondered why he couldn't remember any hugs growing up.

Doctor Legault put a card on the table. "Gentlemen, I can share the details, if you want, or simply sit quietly with you."

"You're saying she's dead," Denis said.

"I am."

"We want to see her."

"We have to," Waine said.

The doctor spread his hands, as if to show they were empty. "She has been gone a long time."

He let them ponder that for a moment. As Waine was drawing breath, he continued, "We have some images of her from her time with us. I can get them for you. They might help you visualize her final year."

Denis nodded. "We want the pictures, yes."

Waine said, "What did you *do* with her?"

"We gave her the best care we could—"

"No. *No.* After she, after she passed. What did you do?"

Denis said, "He's saying was she buried in the ground, or what? Because we all agreed we would be cremated. Do we have to do that, because I don't even know—"

"It's all taken care of," the doctor said. "She was cremated, and her ashes are available. You could, if you want, take them to the family home, or to a favorite place of hers…"

Waine stared at Denis. "Did she have a favorite place? Why don't we know that?"

Denis said, "We'll figure that out. Don't worry about it right now."

The brothers would not meet the doctor's eyes. He sat there with them, but it was not a comforting sit. Finally he said, "There is my card. Call any time if you have more questions or need anything. I will get those images of your sister, and her remains for you."

"And we come back here for them?" Denis said.

"Yes. But call first, please, so I can make sure I am available when you arrive."

Denis nodded. There was so much more to say, and nothing more to say.

Carol Ann Cole

16: Streaking

Hope forgot to tell her mother she was meeting Francis-with-an-i after school and would miss the bus home. She knew she had to be home in time to babysit the twins, though. Mrs. Foss had booked her last week, so it was important.

Francis with-an-i *said* she had arranged a ride home for Hope, but Hope wasn't sure she believed her.

At the last second, Hope changed her mind. She knew she would feel better if she got on the bus as she was supposed to and arrived home on time.

When school was out for the day, Hope was the first student out of her classroom. Streaking, almost in flight, she was heading toward the door to the principal's office. Knowing Francis with-an-i wouldn't be able to argue with her while she was at her desk, Hope slowed down and peeked in to ensure she was there somewhere. She was.

"Hey, Francis with-an-i, I have to go home on the bus today. I forgot I have to babysit the twins for Mrs. Foss so I can't meet up at your apartment. Don't forget to cancel whoever you have lined up to drive me home...very impressive by the way. I couldn't pull that off! Gotta' run. Don't be mad at me."

Hope knew she had said too much, and while she was talking to Francis with-an-i she saw Principal Paul stand up and move closer to the door that separated him from his secretary. He didn't come out, but Hope knew he had heard every word.

For the first time ever, Hope was the first student to jump up into the bus, much to the delight of her bus driver. "Hope, you are *never* first on my bus! This is a treat for me. You're not running away from something are you, honey? Or someone...a young man perhaps?"

Hope attempted a laugh. She knew the bus driver liked to chat with the students, but she was busy watching everyone else who was running for the bus.

She hoped Francis with-an-i did *not* get on the bus and make a fuss, trying to talk her into getting off and going home with her. Hope knew the bus wasn't going anywhere until every student was on board, and she realized, too late, that she could be caught lying. Francis with-an-i told lies all the time, Hope figured, but that didn't mean she should lie. She had to tell a little lie because she did *not* want to go to her apartment, even though she had agreed that, 'today was the day,' whatever that meant. Hope was beginning to regret ever having met Francis with-an-i.

Principal Paul was well liked by everyone, not because he was a pushover but because he was fair, smart and a great basketball player. He made a deal with his students that, as long as everyone remembered to call him Principal Paul during parent-teacher events, they could call him PP during the school day.

Paul heard Hope tell Francis she couldn't, 'meet at her apartment today,' and his antenna went up. She sat directly outside of his office, so he didn't need to raise his voice to speak with her once Hope had disappeared. "Francis, when you finish what you're working on for the day, please join me in my office before you leave."

"Will do, boss-man. I'll be right with you. Give me five."

She knew it! He was going to offer her a teaching position. That's what Francis had applied for and she was extremely well qualified...at least, by her own standards. When she learned there were no immediate teaching positions she had asked about admin-istrative job openings and as she put the plastic cover over her decades-old typewriter she knew she would be glad to be rid of it. She wouldn't mind not sitting right in front of the stuffy school principal's office, either. He had made such a stink about her *not* being known as Francis with-an-i in *his* school that she had agreed to go by Francis. That really irked her, and the second she got her own classroom and her own delicious students she would be Francis with-an-i once again.

"Here I am, Paul. Tell me you have a teaching position for me after all. I can hardly wait." Realizing she was rambling a bit, Francis quickly shut up.

"First things first, Francis. I do not answer to 'boss-man', and don't you ever address me that way again. Now, I do have your file here on my desk, but it's not because I'm about to offer you a teaching position. Sorry to disappoint. Can you remind me why I don't have any references from you yet? You assured me references were on their way and you would bring them to me as soon as they arrived. Not one reference from any of the schools where you have worked in the past, and I see you have worked for several schools, almost changing schools every year or every other year. Why is that?"

Francis was pissed and had to take a deep breath before speaking. "Paul, where is this coming from? I'm doing your lousy secretarial work. I hardly think I need references to do what I'm doing at the moment. So, back to my first question, Where is this coming from?"

Realizing she had used language more colourful than allowed, Francis was tempted to cut her losses and run. But she had bills to pay. "Apologies and all that for calling you boss-man."

"Apology appreciated and accepted. So, thank you for that."

Paul took a pause and opened and closed the file on his desk. He didn't want anything else on the table when he continued with what was really bothering him. "What did Hope Adams mean when she said, 'I can't *meet you at your apartment?*' and why would *any* student be meeting you at your apartment?"

Francis realized she was about to be fired anyway, so, what the Hell, she had nothing to lose. "Why don't you shove this shit-hole school up your ass, Principal Paul? When I'm through with you, no teacher will work for you. I'm going to ruin you." She was yelling but didn't care at this stage.

"You get right back in this office and sit down, young lady. With that filthy mouth you have, I can hardly call you a lady but, please, sit down and prove me wrong. I think all this ranting and raving is because you have something to hide, so I'm going to ask you again. Why was Hope Adams expected to meet you at your apartment after school? What's going on, Francis? Are there serious reasons why you came with absolutely no references? You let me know if you want me to spell any of this out for you."

He let a silence stretch out, like a bowstring tightening. There was nothing she could say.

Finally he nodded. "Please pack up and go home. Be back here in my office at ten tomorrow morning with answers to my questions, or I will have no alternative but to let you go. You call a few of those schools and set up a call for me to get a verbal reference for you until we have the paper copies in your file. For the moment, I want you out of my office and off the school property. Kindly close my door on your way out." Francis slammed the door so hard it rattled, and that was her answer to a couple of Paul's questions. She wouldn't be back in the morning and she did, in fact, have something to hide.

~

Nothing like this had ever happened to Paul in all of his years as a teacher, a vice principal and, for almost a decade, a principal. *The school board will have my ass, as Francis would say, given that I hired the school secretary before receiving her references.*

Paul realized with a chill that there was more to worry about than his own job and his support in the community. He made a note to access Hope's file in the morning to obtain her home phone number. He needed to speak with one of her parents to ensure Francis had not compromised Hope in any way.

17: Lovely Paradise

After a couple drinks at home, Francis with-an-i stretched out and got comfortable on her sofa before she made her call to 'the Cape', as her girlfriend liked to call it. As if everyone should know she was referring to Cape St Mary, the centre of her world.

Francis with-an-i was going to enjoy this little chat. She knew Hope would be babysitting, and that suited her just fine. Her hour-old plan was well thought out and about to drop into place. She reached for her phone and dialed...

"Hello?" came the soft voice.

"Hope, please."

"Hope is unavailable at the moment. Who is calling, please?"

"Oh, that's right, I believe Hope wanted me to call her at the house where she is babysitting. I lost the number for Mrs. Foss, so be a darling and give it to me. Oh, and I don't have all evening so can you hustle a bit, darling?"

"I will do no such thing, and I'm going to go out on a limb and assume I'm speaking with Francis."

"Try again."

"Is this, or is it not, Francis?"

"I identify as Francis with-an-i, and you damn well know it. I assume I'm speaking with the Cape's favourite Private Investigator. Lovely Paradise, you'd be smart to investigate what your darling daughter is up to when she sneaks off to be with me at my apartment. We had plans for today after school, but at the last minute she chickened out, saying something like, 'I'm so disappointed, I have to go home and babysit the brat twins next door. I'll make it up to you next time, I promise. It will be delicious, as you like to call everything about *my* body.'"

Francis with-an-i had to pause for a second to catch her breath. She knew she had nothing left to lose.

"Of course my big boss got involved. If that young and delicious bitch gets me fired, there will be hell to pay."

The soft voice said, "I will be driving Hope to school tomorrow and I will go directly to the principal's office. You might want to skip town before you're arrested for being a predator of young children."

"Not all young children, my dear. Young *female* children, and in particular your delectable Hope."

The phone line went dead.

~

After hanging up, Paradise grabbed a sweater and walked over to have a talk with her daughter. She knew Mrs. Foss wouldn't mind. Paradise would listen to everything Hope offered, but first she owed her girl an apology.

During their flight to Toronto from Honolulu, Hope had asked her mom to talk to her dad about Francis with-an-i. Paradise had discussed this situation with Thomas but somehow they hadn't got around to acting on Hope's behalf. Paradise was upset with herself. Nothing should have been more important than clearing this up before Hope went back to school after summer break.

Hope seems to be involved with this woman. Paradise knew she and Thomas would carry the blame for a lifetime if Francis had taken advantage of their daughter in anyway.

Knocking lightly in case the twins were sleeping, Paradise opened the door. Hope, in tears, was standing there.

She pointed at the receiver of the phone in her hand and whispered, "Mom, it's *her*. She called me, I didn't call her, I promise."

Paradise held our hand and without hesitation Hope passed the phone to her.

"Francis, don't you ever even think of calling my daughter again. Do you understand me?"

"Oh, mommy dearest, I'm shaking in my panties. And, for your information—"

Paradise hung up the phone, not so gently this time.

Then she turned and opened her arms to embrace her sobbing daughter. "I will fix this, sweetheart: I promise you. Your dad and I will visit your school tomorrow morning. We should have been there already, and I'm so sorry we have let you down"

"Oh. My. God. Mom, I'm so sorry. What am I going to do at school tomorrow? I can't face her."

"I have a feeling that that won't be a problem, sweetheart. our dad and I will be right beside you, so you are not to worry about this, okay?"

"Thanks, Mom."

18: The wife was right

"For the last time, Curtis, a wife knows when her husband is unhappy. When are you going to talk to me about this...whatever 'this' is?"

Veronica Curtis had practised what she wanted to say in front of the bathroom mirror every morning after her husband left for work. She had joked with her best friend Diana that she expected the mirror to respond to her eventually.

Diana wanted to help Veronica pack up and move out of the home that Curtis built. "He's married to the police force, Veronica, and that isn't ever going to change. And, my friend, if there is something else going on, why even bother to ask what it is? How do you feel about moving in with me until you figure out your next move?"

Secretly Diana was hoping Veronica would say 'yes' and they could move her out of the house the next time Curtis had a '24 hour shift.' As if...

Curtis knew the wife was right and she was giving him the opening to tell her what was in his heart. Could he really go through with it? How does a man explain to the woman who has been the wife since they were kids just out of high school that he wants out of the marriage? How does he tell her he thinks he has fallen in love with a woman 'down at the station...' A woman who may not have similar feelings for him.

Over several months Veronica made her decision. This was wearing her down and wearing her out. Did her husband really think she was stupid and didn't see the signs that were right in front of her face? So many signs...

Home late every night.

Off to work at the wee hours of the morning.

Extra time spent on personal appearance. (When Curtis took Veronica out she couldn't even get him to remove his baseball hat.)

Pretending to 'just fall asleep' on the sofa. Not intentionally. Sure.

"I've had enough," Veronica whispered with her head in the icebox. She grabbed a second bottle of beer for Curtis and turned the television off before sitting down on the sofa beside her pretending-to-be-napping husband.

"Here's a cold beer to wake you up, my love." Veronica decided the direct line of questioning might be her only chance of getting to the truth. Curtis took the beer but kept his head back on the headrest and his eyes closed.

Veronica pressed on. "I don't know where to start so I've decided to go directly to my last question. Who is she? Who's the other woman in your life? And don't you dare insult my intelligence by pretending you don't understand."

His head was still back but his eyes were open.

"*Who is she?*"

"Paradise."

"*Paradise?* I did *not* see that coming. I knew you were stepping out on me...but with an employee? *Your only female employee?* That's very unprofessional of you, Curtis. How many times have you said that you have no time for office-romance. Don't your practically forbid it? Are the rules different for 'the Sergeant?' You've got some explaining to do."

Curtis bolted to his feet and faced his wife. She could see his pretend-confused look and had a sudden guess who he had been daydreaming about. *No wonder he just blurted out her name. He is going to pay for this.*

"Settle down, woman, and stop jumping to conclusions. I'm having issues with Paradise *on the job*. Nothing personal is going on! I believe she is seeking employment in Halifax, with the Chief Coroner. That woman, I don't know her name, has actually been calling the station trying to find a way to reach Paradise. I didn't think it was my business to share that Paradise had to rush off to Hawaii because of the death of someone connected to her family. I don't know all the details, but even if I did I wouldn't share that information with someone I know nothing about."

"Curtis, I'm not talking about things like her job. I'm talking about Paradise, the woman. I'm sure you've noticed her beauty and her smile for everyone. Christ, even I like the woman and I don't think for one minute she would give you a second glance. So good try, but try again. Who is she? Who are you seeing behind my back? And, do *not* say, 'Paradise' because I know that would not be the truth."

Curtis looked pissed off. "What do you mean, 'Paradise wouldn't give me a second glance'? And how would you know this, anyhow?"

"*That's* where this conversation is headed? You couldn't match up with Paradise even if you left me and put all of your energy into trying to catch her." Veronica couldn't help but chuckle at the absurdity of the thought. She tried, unsuccessfully, to hide her laugh.

Seeing how Curtis seemed so fixated on Paradise, Veronica had another thought. Maybe it was all a fantasy...plain and simple. Veronica thought she better stop insulting her husband, if all he was guilty of was *dreaming* of Paradise...like every other cop at the station.

"I don't appreciate you laughing at me, Veronica. A wife is meant to support her husband, not make fun of him."

"Here's what I'm going to do. We don't talk anyway, so you won't notice I'm gone. I'll pack a bag and leave you to your fantasies for a few days. I'm not running away from our problems or leaving you, Curtis. I need to think about 'us' and I believe you do as well."

"What are you even talking about, woman? Every damn day when I come home from work, who do you think is going to make my supper? Maybe you should think this through. A man needs his supper."

"If I wasn't sure a minute ago, I'm sure now. You make your own damn supper, just like I made mine and ate alone nine out of ten nights when you don't make it home in time."

When Veronica came out of the bedroom with her 'middle size' suitcase packed, Curtis was still standing where she had left him. She waltzed out the side door without even so much as a second glance. She heard him start to protest, and then bite off the words.

~

Several hours later, plus a few extra beers for courage, Curtis decided he best go find Paradise, tell her how he felt and ask about her feelings for him. Maybe she was hoping for this. She could quit the force and maybe work from home. She might like that. Do something that would allow her to be home to make his supper.

Veronica would be sorry she moved out.

One thing at a time, Curtis decided, as he dressed up a bit to impress his new woman. He thought he should take the time to shine his shoes, so he sat back down on the bed. Then he thought he might rest his eyes for a minute or two before heading over to 548 Cape St Mary Road.

Just before passing out, Curtis revelled in the fantasy of being the man Paradise would hold hands with during her early morning walks along Mavillette Beach.

19: Sexual assault

"Paradise, do you *ever* reply to messages left specifically for you?"

Sydney was less than amused that her calls had not been answered...not even after she left her *third* message with Sergeant Curtis at the Cape St Mary police station. She had heard Paradise mention Curtis numerous times and was certain he would have passed her messages on.

"I have no excuse, Sydney, other than to say our lives have turned upside down these last several weeks and months. I made an unplanned trip to Hawaii, and it was not a pleasure trip, I can assure you. When Thomas shared with me what he—"

"With all due respect to your personal life, Paradise, would you mind if we park it until we work through a bit of proposed PI work I have in mind for you?"

"Sydney, you have my complete attention. Go on."

"Good. This case would involve a huge learning curve for you. I will give you all the details I have. Once you have had time to check out some of the details surrounding this case, I hope you will agree to take it on. It's not something I can wade into myself, for personal reasons."

"You're going to have to fill me in, Sydney, because I have no idea what this is about. It's not like you to dance around a request. What, specifically, are you referring to?"

"I'm sure you've heard in the news that a prominent man, living somewhere past the Annapolis Valley and heading towards your area, I believe, has been arrested on several serious charges. Full disclosure: I know this family well, so for personal reasons, that's all I'll give you other than specific details you will need to know about the man charged. More to come, though."

There was quiet on the line. Sydney thought it a good sign that Paradise hadn't jumped in with questions. "Paradise, before we continue, I should have asked if we're on a secure line. Are you at home or work? Is this a good time to talk, or no? This could be a rather lengthy call, and one I hope to have only once. I can't be involved in this case, at least not on a professional level. Personally I will help where I can, though."

"I'm in my office at the police station, and I have all the time you need, so please continue. I will say I assume this does not involve your usual case of 'someone on the slab'"

Sydney thought it best to ignore that comment about the bodies in her morgue. She had caught Paradise off-guard, and she was babbling a little. Good, then. Grab a pen and paper. *Lots* of paper.

As Paradise scribbled to keep up, Sydney shared the story of a sick man, if he was, in fact, guilty as charged. Even if he was not guilty, he would never be rid of the label. 'See that man over there? He was once charged with...'

"My close friend's brother has been charged with three things: Sexual assault. Indecent assault. Gross indecency."

Sydney took her time laying the case out because she didn't want to leave anything unsaid. "I want you to locate your Webster's Dictionary. You will need to understand all three charges and the differences between them. I had to look the three different charges up myself, so that tells you I know next to nothing about a case like this. I will compile data covering legal terms and codes that will give you more detail than you will have found in the dictionary. That's a good place for you to begin though."

Sydney felt honesty was critical. "Paradise, when I was a young child, my friend saved my life. I owe her, and I know it wasn't easy for her to reach out to me for help and guidance."

Sydney sipped her coffee and paused to give Paradise a chance to speak. She hadn't revealed her initial thoughts, but she hadn't said 'no' to taking on the case either.

"Sydney, why me? I wouldn't know where to begin and I'm not sure I could meet your expectations."

"You're a private investigator, for God sake. I'm sure you don't *only* take on the cases you are well versed in. At least think about it, Paradise, and get back to me within a day or two. The family has the funds to pay you to work on this case, and your husband, too, if you need a second PI. The learning curve will be huge. The family is eager to hire fresh eyes because that's what this case needs."

After a lengthening pause, Paradise spoke. Sydney could tell she was intrigued. "I'll get back to you within 48 hours with my decision. I do have time to do a bit of detective work on this. I appreciate your confidence, Sydney, and I welcome this opportunity."

~

Hours later Paradise had written no more than a few sentences and had combed through several volumes of the criminal code.

Sexual assault covers touching another person without their consent when the touching is of a sexual nature. For hundreds of years sexual assault was called rape. Indecent assault is anal intercourse, with the slang term of buggery. The gross indecency offence related to it was repealed in 1988. The buggery offence was re-named 'anal intercourse' and the applicable age of consent was lowered from 21 to 18 years. A second dictionary concluded that gross indecency and indecent assault are similar in the eyes of the law.

A full set of regional and local papers converted to microfiche were kept in the police station with emphasis on articles involving the police. Paradise didn't have to go far, or look for long, to come up with the name of the accused. The victim's name was protected by law which meant he or she was a minor.

As she packed up after a very long evening, Paradise called home. "Thomas, put the coffee on. We've caught a brand new case all wrapped up in 'learning curve' paper, and I'd like to rip the paper off with you. We are both on retainer for 48 hours, and then we have to give Doctor Scott our decision. Do we take the case, or do we say, 'Thanks for considering us but we have to decline'? Full disclosure, Thomas, I think we should take the case."

"One thing at a time, my love. Come home and unwind first. I'll have coffee ready."

Thomas was happy to hear Paradise so excited about what she called a 'learning curve.' The fact that she could include him was a bonus.

20: Lighten up, boys

Her marching orders were hand-delivered to her door late last night. Bonde reviewed the contents and was thankful for the opportunity.

This morning she was to make a call. She knew the drill. Bonde heard the phone ring...almost a full ring. Never a second. This was not her first assignment with 5.0 and she had to smile in spite of herself. This would be fun.

"You've reached 5.0."

Bonde punched in the new code she had received in her package, but didn't say a word.

"Employee contracts. Input your secondary code."

Bonde entered the second code, then just couldn't resist. "You called me, boys, not the other way around, remember? I'm hoping you have a job for me."

"You know that's not how it works, Bonde. *You* talk to us. You received the 5.0 invitation for a contract job at 2.0 under Lieutenant Commander Jalen Lexis. Is this information correct?"

"Lighten up, boys, for God's sake. Yes, that's why I'm calling."

Bonde hoped the work assignment wasn't as dull as the men on the other end of the call. She had no interest in working for the parent company, Hawaii 5.0. Maybe if she could shoot a gun, or even carry an unloaded gun...

"Is that affirmative? Respond with yes or no."

"*Yes.*"

Silently Bonde muttered, *In the name of the Lord, yes!*

And...the call was over. She was disconnected.

Bonde made a mental note to suggest 5.0 offer sensitivity training to their front-line phone team. She would talk with someone at

2.0 and surely they could tell her who to take the idea to.

Bonde had her marching orders. All necessary details (and not a bit more) had arrived in her package. She was to enter the 2.0 warehouse via the rear entrance and ask for Jalen.

Today was her 'Report for Interview' day. She may not like the apparent structure of the job, but Bonde had bills to pay and they were piling up. She was happy to report for duty and grateful for the opportunity.

~

Jalen had made sure to have Bonde arrive during Lenny's shift so he could introduce the two. If all went well, she would begin work immediately. By the time anyone arrived at 2.0 for their 'interview' they had already been hired. The only thing Jalen could find in Bonde's record that bothered him was her use of foul language.

He would never say it aloud, but a man swearing didn't seem as offensive as it did coming from a woman's lips. It cheapened a wo-man in some way. This was Jalen's opinion only and he was careful with whom and how he shared this particular line of thinking. Given the comments about this in Bonde's file, Jalen was prepared to address this in their first meeting. Delicately...he kept reminding himself he would need to speak to this delicately.

"Bonde, I assume? I've been watching for you." Extending a hand, Jalen continued. "Lieutenant Commander Jalen Lexis, and within the walls of this warehouse I prefer that all of my team call me Jalen." He paused as they completed a two-pump handshake. "Welcome aboard the 2.0 team, young lady."

He could see her eyes flicker over him, and register approval. Well, that was fine, but he hoped she would keep her opinions to herself. "I'll give you a tour of the operation, introduce you to a few of the men—you're our only female team member by the way—and the tour will end in our lounge, where your teammate for the night shift will join us."

"*Christ almighty*, my first shift will be tonight? What about the interview?"

"You're not prepared to work tonight or you are unwilling to work tonight? Which is it?"

"Gentle Jesus, man, slow down. Who was supposed to tell me to bring my pajamas and toothbrush? Maybe your connection with 5.0 isn't as good as it should be because they told me when and where to arrive *for my interview* and that was it. And I might add, every damn 5.0 voice I have spoken with seemed to have his attitude shoved up his ass."

Jalen put a hand up. "I'm going to stop you right there and point out a few things that, quite frankly, make me rethink having you join our team. Foul language is not a sign of strength. You exhibit weakness when you begin every sentence that comes out of your mouth with a cuss word."

He could see he was upsetting her, so he decided on a different approach. He stood up and motioned for her to follow him.

"Change of plans, Bonde. The job is yours if you want it, but how about you report for duty tomorrow rather than today? If that works for you, I'll take you directly to our lounge and have Len meet us there. Len will take you through the warehouse and describe his job, which is also your job. It feels like we are getting off on the wrong foot and I take responsibility for that. If this works for you, perhaps you could share your designs for an entire revamped 5.0 another time. How does that sound?"

Jalen used his number three smile, the sincere one, and saw Bonde relax a bit.

"I've been told I have a foul mouth so damn many times I should know better. I regret the way I spoke, I apologize and guarantee it won't happen again. You have my word. Now, kind sir, take me to Len. *Please.*"

"I'll hold you to that, Bonde."

~

A voice inside Bonde's head whispered urgently. *Please do hold me to that...what I wouldn't like to do to you, Lieutenant Commander.'*

She followed in her new boss's wake, keeping up as best she

could and admiring his rear elevation as he strode along. She wondered if Jalen was always in a rush, or if this related simply to his wanting to pass her over to Len.

21: Suicide note

~~Dearest Hope,~~
~~Paradise,~~
~~Principal Paul,~~
Why in God's name can't I at least decide to whom I want to gift my 'fare thee well' letter?

When I manage to put my thoughts on paper, thought Francis-with-an-i and not for the first time, *my words have to be memorable for a very long time. I do not want to be forgotten. I have already created an opportunity to spew my venom to those deserving of it and now I sit with one final task. It's time I write my letter.*

The floor was covered with crumbled sheets of paper, every one with a few more words than the last. Yet she was not comfortable with exactly what she wanted to say *or* whom she wanted to say it to.

Best to keep it simple, Francis with-an-i thought. And her thoughts were dark...very dark.

"If I'm serious about this I need to leave a note." Saying it out loud made it real. She *was* going to do this. "Today is the day."

In a rather strange way Francis with-an-i was excited by the possibilities of what the day might bring and what her ending might say to those who shunned her.

Writing 'to whom-it-may-concern,' might have to work since she had already crossed through the three salutations she had considered. She knew that putting her thoughts on paper first would tell her whom she was writing to. Who was she kidding? Francis with-an-i knew exactly whom she would select to read her final thoughts.

Finally, and only after finishing a six-pack of beer, two of her remaining four joints and some chocolate, Francis with-an-i knew she would write to Hope. If that changed after she finished her letter, she would start again.

It wasn't as if she had a job to get to...thanks to Paradise, who had ruined everything. *That bloody bitch*, she thought.

>*To my young love,*
>
>*I write my final letter to you, my darling Hope, knowing that for a fleeting moment you acknowledged being a greenhorn in bed. Your attempt at making your thoughts and feelings appear to be rather ho-hum didn't fool me for a second. At first I thought your behaviour was somewhat asinine, but, keeping it simple for your young mind, I think you know your performance in my tiny home was disaster-ish. Sub-par. Only one of us was naked, as you will remember. That's not how sex works, my young love. Oh how I wish I could stay on this earth long enough to show you how to love me. First I would teach you how to love you.*
>
>*Hope, my love, gay, dyke, lesbian, transgender and queer are all terms I have been called and I had hoped to discuss my past life with you. I'll come back to this later.*
>
>*Our first night together turned sexual before we talked. I wanted to understand what you know about gays and lesbians. All of us who fall under one of these names understand we will not speak of it outside our safe place. For me, that's my apartment.*
>
>*It's actually stronger than saying 'we will not think of it...' Perhaps it should be 'we dare not think of it...' Hope, it's dangerous for me to speak of my sexuality in public. That is a fact and it's heartbreaking. I feel I have to hide the real me. Every damn morning before I leave the house I remind myself to keep my sexuality silent when out in public.*
>
>*I trusted you almost immediately. I liked the visual package you presented when you walked into the diner. You had 'newbie' all over your face. I like that face! Sounds shallow of*

me now, but I couldn't help lusting over you the second I laid my eyes on you. All you wanted to talk about was the ongoing fight you were having with your mother. I turned that to my advantage and agreed with everything you said. I know that made you feel rather grownup. You helped me dislike your mother almost instantly and I don't even remember what you two were fighting about. I do remember it wasn't as import-ant an issue as you were suggesting, but I didn't want to dis-agree with you on anything. At least not until I got you na-ked. Sorry, my mind keeps going back to the sex we did not have.

Watch out for your mother, Hope. Paradise didn't impress me one little bit, and she was not thinking of you when she forced us apart. If I had had a gun that night your mother would be dead.

Do you realize that bitch cost me my job? I needed that job and Paradise pranced right into PP's office and said you did not want me 'pestering' you. PP likely told her that he had already decided to fire my ass, but I could have talked that man into keeping me working just outside of his office. He liked the view. I know he did. I caught him checking me out a few times.

Hope, your mother is a Bitch.... However, my letter isn't about her so I'll try to focus on 'us' now.

Could there have been an 'us', Hope? I would have loved trying, and part of me wants to stick around and try to win you over. But I'm sick of this entire freaking world. It's not all on you, my young beauty. Deep down I know you're not gay.

My deep and negative attitude began a long time ago, when I developed a crush on a girl in my high school class. I shared my feelings in confidence and I thought she under-stood this was to go no further. She promised she would tell no one. The next morning the word 'dyke' was written on my locker door. She said she didn't do it, but she clearly had been talking about me. Probably laughing at me, too. Lesbians are always getting laughed at and I'm tired of being treated like a freak. We can't even be ourselves when we're out in public. That better change one of these days. I'll be dead and buried, but I hope the view of women like me changes for those who come after me.

Francis with-an-i realized her thoughts were all over the place. Maybe she was thinking too much.

Once I finish my letter, my darling Hope, I will mail it to you marked personal and confidential. Then I will go to where I'm going.

Be happy, Hope, but be your own person. I know you're very young and yes I know I'm much older than you. I loved you regardless of our age difference and in your heart of hearts I believe you loved me. I need that to be my final thought as I leave this earth. Surely you won't begrudge me that?

By the time this note reaches you in Cape St Mary I will have been found hanging from my own clothes line. Hung out to dry.

Apologies for my humour.

To say I will love you forever doesn't ring true, so I will say I will love you for my time on this earth. That sounds cold, but I'm guessing taking my own life will be even colder.

I remember you removing your top for me, during our first and only real night of passion. It was lovely, wasn't it? I'm saddened that it ended before I was able to make love to you. It ended before it began.

Forever and ever it will be you, Hope. Only you.

With all my love,

Francis with-an-i.

PS I apologize in advance for the hullabaloo my suicide will create. Perhaps some will even learn from it. We're all different and by the grace of God we are all worth something. I hold no grudge against those too small-minded to know me and give me a chance at life.

22: The charge was rape

Paradise and Thomas left the Cape in the darkness of an early morning, en route to Halifax. They were off to give a status report to Doctor Scott.

The charge was rape. The accused was known by name. The victim was known as Child X. They had only bad news to share and they had lots of it.

First stop was in the town of Lawrence to refill their coffee cups and their gas tank. Only minutes passed before they were back in the car. They had already decided where they would stop for an early lunch. A bright and cheerful sign said, 'Welcome to Kentville' and they were happy to explore.

Over greasy burgers with fries and more coffee than they needed they reviewed their file.

"Thomas, I'm glad we gave the accused as much of our time as we gave the victim. We did some deep investigating and that uncovered the very thing Doctor Scott hoped we would not find."

"I hear you loud and clear," Thomas said. "We are not paid to take sides. We're paid to be thorough investigators who always keep an open mind."

"We sure are learning as we go," Paradise offered.

"Do you think Doctor Scott will continue to be your friend when we share what we have learned about her long-time-friend's brother, *the accused?*"

Paradise frowned in thought. "She's a professional. She hired us as professionals. I don't think she can expect us to sugar-coat our findings."

"I know you and Sydney have become close," Thomas whispered. "It would appear she blatantly neglected to give us some facts about this case. Facts that would have been helpful to have some time ago. I would like to take the lead at least in the early stages of our presentation. Can you live with that?"

"Sure," Paradise said with a smile.

Back in the car, Thomas stuck his head into the map while Paradise got them back on the road. "Now to figure out how to get there."

Paradise let him ponder and growl at the map while she drove them out of the Valley and made the turn toward Halifax. But after he had crumpled the map up and smoothed it out a couple of times, she said, "Given that Sydney invited us to her home rather than her office, she must be desperate for this case to never be connected to her in any way."

"I know. But that's out of our hands. I mean, we won't go giving newspaper interviews, but everybody in the legal system loves having a juicy secret to share with their friends." They rode on, mostly in silence, until the road made its transition from country highway to part of the city.

"Good Lord," Paradise said, "I have never been anywhere in Halifax other than the jail, the Chief Coroner's office and the hotel I stayed in. This is huge compared to the Cape!"

"You managed Honolulu," Thomas said, glancing from the map to the streets and buildings that flitted past. "This is just a big village in comparison."

He gave her directions to turn here, and take that corner, mostly in time for her to do it without screeching the tires. And then he was silent, peering at street signs.

"Tell me you haven't gotten us lost with only ten minutes to spare."

"Oh ye of little faith," Thomas said with a big smile. "Slow down just a bit and turn left at the second set of lights."

"Second set of lights."

"Actually turn left here between the lights."

"Thomas!"

"Sorry." But he didn't look sorry. "Check out the size of these homes, Paradise. And hers is just up ahead. That rather large mansion on the left...white with a brilliant red door and matching red trim on the house."

"Can't be."

"Yes it can and it is," Thomas replied.

Paradise attempted to pull into the rather small driveway. "Nobody needs a home this size!"

"Is that your friend, standing in the open door?"

"Gentle Jesus."

"Language."

"Did I say that out loud?"

Paradise was smiling and nodding at Sydney. She couldn't help but wonder if they would remain friends. The PIs were armed with more detail than Sydney might have expected they would uncover in the early stages of their work.

"Welcome, Paradise. Welcome to my home. And you must be Thomas? I have heard so much about you."

"Oh. My. God. Sydney, you live in a palace. And when I was in your office I was going on and on about our little home in the Cape!"

"Our home in the Cape *is our little palace*," Thomas said. "And we have the sounds of the ocean outside our windows, while Sydney has commuters."

"I've made lunch, not knowing if you would have eaten," Sydney said as she ushered them into the broad, cool hallway. "Do you have time for us to eat and then work after that, or are you in a rush to return home?"

Thomas sent a glance at Paradise: *Take the lead on this.*

"You know what, Sydney," she said, "it's not so much that we are in a rush but, speaking for myself, I'm a nervous wreck over what we are about to share with you. I would like to lay it all out rather than pretend I'm comfortable having a leisurely lunch. So I hope you haven't gone to a lot of trouble with a meal and everything."

Sydney looked fixedly at her for a long moment, then nodded. "So you've figured it all out," she said. "I guess I knew you would."

Paradise started to say three different apologies and decided saying none of them was wiser.

"Let's go into the family room, then," Sydney said. "Or, rather, you go on in and get yourselves settled. I'll just fetch a couple of trays."

The family room could have seated a family of ten. Thomas and Paradise choose chairs near a broad coffee table where they could spread out papers if they needed to. Sydney also loaded the table up with trays of food and all the clutter of silverware and clinking glasses that should have heralded a carefree meal.

She took several trips to get everything in place, and then fussed about arrangements for a bit, as if the precise placement of each serviette was the key decision of the day.

"Sydney, please sit," Paradise finally said. "I think you're more nervous than we are."

"All right, then." Sydney took a seat on the opposite side of the table from her two PIs. "All right. Say the thing."

"Thomas and I have decided to give you our closing comments first, but I promise we will then fill in all the blanks. Feel free to interrupt at any time if you have questions." She tapped a little stack of paper. "We have a printed copy of our notes that we will leave with you."

23: Show time

Paradise and Thomas were a true tag team. Without a word spoken they were able to comfortably move back and forth and could finish each other's sentences.

Now they gave each other their best *show time* look and Paradise began. "Sydney, thank you for trusting Thomas and me to investigate this case on your behalf. You can be absolutely assured that no one was aware of who we were working for or what we were looking for in the research library. We spoke to no one about this and not once did we meet outside of our own home to discuss the details."

As Paradise took a deep breath, Thomas jumped in. "As I understand it, the accused is a friend of yours. Is this correct, Sydney?"

"Not true," said Sydney, surprising both PIs. "Paradise, I told you I was a friend of the family, not specifically with the accused. I have never told you I was a friend of his. I don't know why you would say that."

Clearly Sydney was upset and they were just beginning their presentation!

"If I remember correctly, Paradise, I told you the accused is a *brother* of my friend. That's all I said about him, so please don't make that particular mistake again."

Thomas sat down but remained in direct eye contact with her. Paradise knew this was his strong suit so she remained quiet.

"Duly noted," he said. "We apologize, and will not repeat that mistake. Now, if you could hear me out we would appreciate it. It's important that we have every fact 100% correct. Some facts will bring back memories and emotions you would rather forget. We know that. You have hired us to conduct an investigation and that's what we are doing."

Thomas paused because Sydney was on her feet, pacing back and forth in front of them. "I know what I hired you to do, Thomas, so, for God's sake, please start stating facts or this meeting is over."

Paradise was a bit stunned. She hardly knew the woman standing in front of her. "Remember, I'm your friend, Sydney, and Thomas is my PI partner here today. Please show some respect for the work we do. I'm asking you to sit down. *Please sit down.*" Paradise had to dig deep to keep her own feelings at bay.

After a long pause, Sydney sat on the edge of her seat, as if she might flee at any moment.

Thomas began again. "Sydney, we have learned that you were barely in high school when you had an affair with a married man. You got pregnant before your sixteenth birthday. This person took you to a back-alley abortion clinic. You climbed a fire escape to enter the clinic. Your friend paid for your 'procedure' in advance, and when it was over he had disappeared."

Thomas paused for corrections, but Sydney stayed silent. She was looking down at her hands, which were clenched together and resting on her lap.

"As you tried to walk down the spiral staircase you had to sit on every step until you were able to manage the pain and take one more step. Finally, with your feet on the ground you looked for your friend and his car and realized you were going to have to walk home. Your parents met you at the door ready to punish you for not coming home immediately after school. Instead, they put you to bed and took care of you, no questions asked."Sydney said, "What does something from my youth have to do with this investigation? The incident in question happened only months ago. Not millions of years ago."

Paradise wanted to give Sydney a hug before she began. However, Thomas had warned her time and again to not let personal feelings or emotions creep into her work.

She took a breath to get herself under control, then said, "Thomas and I have studied all of this. What happened when you were a fifteen-year-old child is eerily similar to the actions of this investigation. It's possible that it might be up to you to speak up on this case, Sydney. Sorry, I'm getting ahead of myself. Please let me continue to present what we think we know so you can correct us if we are going wrong."

After a taut moment, Sydney nodded.

"When you realized you were still pregnant, you went in search of this man who had captured your fascination. He would help you, you were certain of it. Better to tell him rather than your parents. The details of your search are in our report. However, we know this monster (I know that's just an opinion) tried to rape you although your were clearly pregnant. When you finally went to your parents for help, you learned it was much too late to have an abortion. They sent you away in shame, to a distant 'aunt', where you delivered a healthy baby. Sydney, we were unsure if you would want us to learn details following the birth. We can pick up that thread and continue, but we wanted you to know what we have uncovered to date. You don't look surprised by anything we have said thus far."

Paradise took a drink of her coffee to break the thought process for a second.

As she did, Sydney stood again. "Please excuse me for a few minutes. Don't leave. I'll be back when I can converse with some decorum of sanity. Reliving these details, and they are all correct, has made me feel quite ill."

With that Sydney silently left the room.

"Are you thinking what I'm thinking?" Paradise whispered to Thomas.

"My heart hurts, Paradise, honest to God. We didn't shock her, but I'd be willing to bet we broke her heart. Sydney is an intelligent woman...she knows what's coming, don't you think?"

Paradise simply nodded.

24: The X Mrs.

"That did *not* work out as I had hoped!"

Sergeant Curtis was shouting at his reflection in the bathroom mirror. "I didn't give the wife credit. She was damn smart about everything and when I told her I had good news, *she could come back home,* she shared her own plans for the first time."

Her words seared his memory.

I'm moving out permanently, Curtis. I'm leaving you and I hope Paradise kicks you to the curb. Perhaps then you will stop and reflect on the life we had. I had no idea you were unhappy with me. With us. I'll be back to pick up the rest of my things, to discuss who keeps the antique furniture we collected, and how we split our bank account and all of our investments. Our portfolio looks good...do you even know that?

Veronica walked out on Curtis that day and he hadn't heard a word from her or about her. He had checked every house in the Cape and her car was nowhere. Nobody seemed to know where she had gone. If Curtis found out that anyone in the Cape had helped her escape her own husband, he would raise holy hell, and he made sure everyone knew it.

She has to be somewhere.

"Veronica Curtis had plans, all right, and they don't include me. For God's sake, she's my wife. *My* wife."

Enough talking to the bathroom mirror. Curtis tried to change his mood. It was too early in the morning to be this ugly.

Before Paradise and Thomas left for Halifax, Curtis had a long talk with her. "A private contract with a very private individual," was all Paradise would share about their plans. The minute she mentioned the word 'private' Curtis had the confidence to spill his own news with her. Perhaps with a bit too much detail.

Thinking he would throw out a bone, so to speak, Curtis had visited Paradise at her desk late one evening. He wanted to make the conversation personal, and if he went to her, then she couldn't get up and leave.

"Paradise what would you say if I told you I might have big plans for you and me by the time you return from the city. Big plans."

Her response didn't fit in with his plans at all. "Great idea, boss, Thomas and I have personal plans that I hope to share with you by the time we return. We have made *big plans* as a couple—"

"Let me guess. You and Thomas are splitting up? I knew it. I just knew it by the way you were listening to me the other day in my office when I shared that Veronica had moved out. You were leaning in to me and I know you were feeling something for me. Am I right?"

Paradise knew she hadn't really been paying attention because the home life of the person you report to shouldn't be your business. At least that's what she thought. Knowing her *convent years* hampered her somewhat when engaging in personal situations, Paradise tried to think back to the exact conversation and couldn't remember it all. Clearly she had checked out mentally at the first negative comment about his wife. Paradise liked Veronica very much and wondered some days when she dropped in to see Curtis during the day why she never appeared happy.

Trying to teach the wife a lesson, Curtis had to admit Veronica administered the final blow. He didn't see it coming.

~

Just up the line, in a small town much bigger than Cape St Mary, Veronica Curtis had rented a tiny studio apartment. It was all she really needed for now, while she rediscovered who she was and what she wanted in her life.

First thing, Veronica would like to find a job. She was open to whatever paid her bills for now. Her lawyer had warned her to take her share of money out of her joint account with Curtis. She didn't think that would be an issue...but would it? Would her husband think so little of her that he would take money that didn't belong only to him?

Her lawyer didn't know her husband. Curtis was a cheat, or he wanted to be, but he was not unkind. Surely to God she wasn't married to a thief!

At thirty-six, Veronica still had hopes to become a mother. But her clock was ticking.

"This could get complicated," she shared with her first new friend in Middleton.

Her landlords were Mr. P and Irene. From the first day she knocked on their door to ask if it was true that they had a small place she could rent she felt the weight of her world fall off of her tiny shoulders.

"First month is free," Mr. P had said. "You make sure you like us and we will do the same."

Veronica felt comfortable from day one sharing with her landlords that, in fact, her husband was the Police Sergeant in Cape St Mary and she was worried that he would have no problem finding her.

"Every family has problems. Don't you worry about that because it won't bother us one bit," Irene said as she reached out to hug their first tenant. "There's nothing to you, dear, so I'm going to invite you over for a bit of Mr. P's Italian cooking. Starting today... supper is in one hour. Please join us. We always have enough food to feed at least one more person and you are welcome at our table."

Then Mr. P shared a thought. "Veronica, rather than the parking spot that I just said was yours, I'm moving you to the spot just behind the house. That puts you closer to your entrance to the studio. More important, though, your car will not be visible to drive-by traffic. Just in case your husband comes driving by.

25: Abandoned child

Sydney returned to Paradise and Thomas totally gutted, and knowing that the worst blow was still to come. She couldn't take in any more information until she had some alone time and, if possible, some sleep.

"With apologies, could I ask you to stay in Halifax tonight, at my expense of course? I'll have hot coffee on anytime after 7 tomorrow morning."

Sydney was looking at Paradise, who was looking at Thomas, who responded. "You're paying the bills, Sydney, so you make the decisions. We'll be here at seven tomorrow."

In silence Thomas gathered their papers, and the PIs left to search for a hotel room for the night. Sydney watched from a window in a darkened room as they stopped and seemed to argue. Paradise was gesturing back toward the house, and Thomas indicating the open car door.

With relief she saw Thomas prevail. He waited until Paradise was seated, then went around to the driver's side. She was ready to flinch back out of sight, but he didn't glance back at the house. Sydney didn't allow her tears to fall until she saw the taillights of their car disappear as they turned left and out of view.

~

From all appearances, morning came early for everyone. The front door opened the second Thomas turned their car into Sydney's driveway. "I don't see her. Do you, honey?"

"No," Paradise whispered, thinking in some way Sydney might hear their conversation. "Let's assume she opened the door for us, not a burglar. So we'll let ourselves in and head to her kitchen for our first coffee of the day."

As they walked toward the house, Thomas placed his hand on the small of her beautiful back and murmured, "*All business* today. Remember, no small talk until we signal to each other that this presentation is behind us."

"It's going to be a rough day for her."

"Remember what we discussed? Sydney, most likely, knows what we are going to say. We will simply be confirming her suspicions."

Paradise stopped for a quick moment on the top step of Sydney's front porch. "She is going to hear us tell her the man who probably fathered her child is a rapist, and more. Oh. My. God."

Still with his hand on her back Thomas ushered Paradise inside and directly to the kitchen.

"Good morning you two. I was sure you would easily follow the smell of coffee, and here you are."

Sydney seemed nervous. She looked dishevelled, with both eyes swollen, probably from too many tears. Both Paradise and Thomas poured large mugs of coffee but declined the offered muffins.

"Okay, well, maybe at break time then?"

Thomas could see Sydney was trying hard to make this personal. He led the way to the living room, speaking as he went. He could hear the two women following him. "Sydney, Paradise and I hope we are bringing this news to you in the best possible way. We talked at length about wanting to protect your privacy, and I assure you we have done exactly that as we collected the facts."

He waited until the others had chosen seats, then sat so he could look from one to the other easily. "Interrupt me at any time to ask questions, or if you need a break."

"Thank you Thomas. I feel pretty much as bad as I look this morning and, honestly, I almost cancelled. However, I gave myself a slap upside the head, and here we are."

She gave a little smile, and Thomas resisted returning one. This was not the moment for that. "Sydney we will be using the terms 'accused' and 'child X,' and, similar to yesterday, we will leave a paper copy of this presentation with you."

"Okay."

"The accused has a history of sexual assault. This may be news to you. It may also be news to your friends. They may have no idea of the predatory actions this man has been accused of. He has never gone to court, but that was more about parents not wanting their children to be put through all that. A couple of times the process went through discovery and the prosecutors were ready to go, but the child in question wanted it to all go away and didn't want to talk about it further. That's as close as the accused has come to a court process."

Paradise said, "The accused has gotten off lucky, Sydney. I interviewed the mother of Child X and she gave me what we need to understand what is to come. On a lovely summer's day Child X ran home, supporting her broken arm with her other hand. All she said at first was that a man hurt her arm because she wouldn't get into his truck. And her arm hurt...'really really bad.' She was eleven years old. *Eleven*."

Thomas could see this was news to Sydney.

Paradise continued, "The parents took her to the hospital, of course. The child had blood on the back of her skirt, a bloody nose, and, of course, the broken arm. At the hospital, an emergency room doctor and a surgeon cared for Child X. A policeman took the parents into another room to hear their story. Remember, at this point, nothing was certain. But at a certain point the officer requested a team experienced in sexual assault."

Paradise picked up her coffee cup, and Thomas took over. He stood, looking directly at Sydney, who seemed to shrink back into her chair. "Child X had been raped. The accused had been brutal, and the child required surgery to repair a tear in the vaginal wall. She may never be able to carry a child. We spoke recently with the mother of Child X and confirmed that a therapist is working with her on the non-physical injuries."

Sydney appeared to be losing control once again. Her voice was tense as she asked, "Thomas, how do they know it was this man in particular? What makes you think these are facts?"

"The accused has a history, so he's in the police system. He seems to break one arm of each victim, probably so they can't fight back, or leave scratch marks on his face or arms. He has always lived in the area. His wife divorced him when she learned the accused had had an affair with a fifteen-year-old that produced a child"

Bursting into tears, Sydney ran from the room and up the stairs.

After a moment, Thomas nodded. "She knew. Just like you said."

Paradise rose and, following their plan, went up the stairs. She made enough noise that Sydney would hear her coming. If the bedroom doors were closed, she would return to the living room.

~

A bedroom door was wide open. Paradise could see Sydney sitting on the edge of the bed, looking down at nothing. She stepped into the room and stood just inside the door.

"Sydney, we believe, from what we have uncovered, that that fifteen-year-old was you. It was you who tried to get an abortion and thought you had succeeded, correct? This monster paid for you to go to a butcher. He cut your flesh to create lots of blood and told you it was done. Months later, when you realized you were still pregnant, you went to your mother. And she instantly shipped you off so she wouldn't have to feel the shame or the gossip of her circle."

Sydney looked up. "Paradise, I have to know. Did my child live? Is he or she okay? I'm so sad to admit I don't even know the sex of my child. My 'Aunt' ran a home for unwed mothers. Her place was packed while I was there. We did all the work in the house and she got paid for it. She was not kind to us, but we stuck up for each other and helped others with chores once ours were complete."

Paradise gave Sydney a glass of water and rubbed her back as she took a few sips. She knew her friend needed a minute or two before she could continue.

"Paradise, the day I went into labour I walked to the hospital myself. I gave birth two days later and the next day I was forced to

leave the hospital. I walked back to the home, knowing I had aban-
doned my child. They wouldn't even let me see my baby. 'It's better
this way' is what we always heard. One of my friends who was almost due to deliver her own baby offered to be with me in the op-
erating room and to clean up after me. We thought this would give
her access to my child even for a moment or two, but this did not
happen."

Sydney made a helpless gesture. "I never saw her again. We
weren't old enough or smart enough to remember to get phone
numbers or a mailing address. Last names were forbidden in the
home, maybe so we couldn't contact each other and compare facts
about what really went on at my 'Aunt's house. Oh Paradise, I made
so many mistakes back then."

Sydney put her head in her hands and wept.

Some time passed in silence before she said she felt comfortable
enough to go back downstairs. "Poor Thomas must be feeling left
out. Let's join him before he comes looking for us."

Slowly the two women made their way back to the living room,
after stopping in the kitchen to get three glasses and a large
pitcher of ice-cold water.

As they were getting settled, Thomas flashed Paradise a questioning glance and she answered with raised eyebrows and a nod.

Paradise said, "Sydney, you asked about your child. We did not
investigate the baby. We tried to stay true to your initial request.
You asked us to bring you facts about the accused, and that's been
our goal today."

Thomas stood, signalling he would step in. "Sydney, Child X and
her mother are telling the truth. The medical records confirm this.
The family knows who the accused is, but he lives far enough away
from them that they mainly just know *of* him. The child easily
picked his face out of nine pictures the police asked her to look at."

"How terrible for that girl."

"There is one more proof," Thomas said. "It involves something
called deoxyribonucleic acid, or DNA. Why it is important requires
a bit of an explanation, so this might be a good place to break for
lunch."

"Oh, God, yes, I need a break."

Sydney led the way to the, kitchen where her housekeeper had lunch all prepared.

"I don't know how much of an appetite I have," she said, but Paradise noticed her surrounding her meal with evident pleasure.

When she had regained some of her normal poise, Sydney turned to Thomas with a mock-stern look. "Oh, by the way, young man, I'm familiar with DNA, in all its coils and revelations, in my line of work."

26: DNA was new

Trying to keep a straight face, Thomas began again about forty-five minutes after their lunch break. "DNA is very new in our line of work, and may require an in-depth explanation for Paradise and me, but clearly not for our Chief Coroner."

The three shared a smile. Then Thomas continued, "All kidding aside, Sydney, it's very clear. Evidence collected from the body of our eleven-year-old Child X points to the accused. A broken arm is something the accused has used time and time again to disarm his young prey. The police generally have kept that out of the media so that copycats wouldn't try the same thing. It's him, Sydney. And the prosecution will have even more evidence against him."

Paradise leaned forward. "Sydney, there is no doubt this man is guilty. Child X will hold up in court and the accused will be put away for a very long time. I know he is a part of your own youth, but we advise you, as strongly as we can, to stay away. He's a monster, and if you go to him trying to learn if he has information about the child you had together, his legal team will find a way to bring this 'bombshell news' into court. It could ruin you and taint the case against him. When all of this is settled, Thomas and I would be happy to help you find your child. But...you must separate this accused man's trial from finding your child. Don't go there, even in your head, until this trial concludes. Can you do that, Sydney?"

There was a long pause. Then Sydney raised her head. "I can."

~

In a modest home just down past lower Middleton, the black phone mounted on the kitchen wall was ringing.

Carol Ann Cole

"Does anybody want me to answer this ear-blasting phone?" the man shouted at the world in general.

As he was about to answer it Liz ran into the room and snatched the receiver from his hand. "Good God, man, what have I told you? This is a private phone. What part didn't you understand the last time we discussed you *not* answering my phone?"

"I said 'hello' to whoever is calling you. I didn't realize answering your phone is a crime."

She grabbed the mile-long cord and sat down in the family room. She was hoping it was Sydney calling.

"Hello?" Liz wasn't sure if her house guest had left the kitchen area so she kept her voice just above a whisper.

"Hi Liz, it's Sydney, and it sounds like it's a bad time. Does that voice belong to *him*? If so, I don't want to keep talking."

"Let me stick my head into the kitchen and see...nope he's gone. I see him walking out towards his car, so he's likely off somewhere."

Liz returned to her comfortable chair. "What did your private eye tell you? Anything suggesting I should keep him out of my home?"

"Liz, the first thing you must promise me is that you will not allow him into your home again, especially when your grandchildren are visiting...both male and female."

"Well, that tells me everything then, doesn't it?"

Liz immediately regretted her angry tone. "I'm sorry, please forgive me. Yes, I promise and I'm thinking I won't let him rent a room from me any longer, either."

"That's a very wise decision. My PIs just left. I'm not sure I should share all of the details over the telephone, so if I can't get down to see you in the next week or two, do you want to come to my place for a girls' night? I'll make sure we have your favourite meal for dinner and you know I'll be out the door and off to work long before you awake, so you can just lock the front door on your way out."

"I'll come into the city. I appreciate how busy you are. How about tomorrow evening?"

98

"The sooner the better, I think. So I'll save the rest until then."

"Well, but tell me *something* about him, either related to this case or prior to."

"Sure. I'll give you a few facts in rapid fire," Sydney said. "You can ask all the questions you want when we are together. First, get him out of your house."

"Okay."

Second, don't make notes of things we discuss...leave no paper trail at all."

"That serious?"

"He's a rapist. He's a pedophile. He has a long list of charges but nothing has stuck...yet."

Liz felt cold, as if all her blood had retreated to the very inner-most core of her body.

"He prefers little girls but doesn't turn away from little boys. Child X is eleven years old and has been scarred for life, in more ways than one."

"Dammit."

"Last one for now," Sydney said. "He knows me, so it's vitally important that he never ever connects the dots."

There was a long pause. Then Liz managed a shaky sigh. "Details over dinner tomorrow evening, then. I'll bring the wine and some comfy clothes."

"No wine, Liz. You know my rule. I *always* supply the wine."

Liz knew there was no point in saying goodbye. Sydney had already hung up.

~

Sydney wanted to call the bastard to ask about *their* child. But she already knew he didn't give a damn about her or about her baby. She was surprised that she could still feel the sting so many years after the incident.

The day she realized she was *still* pregnant Sydney had gone to his office and waited by his car to talk to him. She'd had nowhere to go and no one to talk to. She tried to hide her baby bump by standing on the passenger side of his car.

She could see him leaving the office. He was coming towards her. He almost pounced on her as he reached his car. "You little bitch. You kept my money and didn't have the abortion?"

"How can you say that? You drove me to 'your good friend' who owed you a favour. You know I had the procedure. You even drove me home with all that blood in your fancy car. You went berserk when you spotted the blood on the seat."

He grabbed for her, but Sydney backed away. She did not even know this monster.

He noticed other people walking out of the building, and stepped away from her, adjusting his jacket. "I bet the kid wasn't even mine. You won't get one penny out of me."

"But—"

"I suggest you take off, or I will run over you and your bastard kid. I swear to God."

"I'm begging you, please help me. I'm homeless and our baby is due in a month."

"All the more reason to drive over you. I swear to God," he hissed, "you won't ruin my life."

"Please," was all Sydney could say. Then he was gone in a squeal of tires.

That was the last word she had ever spoken with him.

Her mother did not know she had gone to him before reaching out to her. It didn't matter, though. Even her own mother disowned her.

27: Hold on, cowboy

"Well, knock me down and call me Susan, what are the chances?" Bonde was off and running the second she laid eyes on Len, leaving the Lieutenant Commander scratching his head. He had no idea why she reacted the way she did and he wasn't sure Len would either.

"The two of you know each other?"

"Well...we are *about* to know each other. Len, I have wanted to meet you just to shut the Lieutenant Commander up, if nothing else." Bonde turned and smiled at the big boss but he was not smiling in return.

Turning back to Len, she went on, thinking it couldn't get any worse. "They call me Bonde and, by God, you look exactly like a fella I met, or tried to meet, recently on a flight. Is that even possible?" The bad vibes Bonde was getting from the big boss wouldn't give her a break. Not for a second.

Jalen spoke up. "You're to call me Jalen when we are all working together inside this warehouse. Do you understand that?"

With a pretend salute, Bonde clicked her heels together and replied, "Yes, sir."

"Bonde, we also talked about your potty mouth, but it sounds like you will need a refresher course in what we do and don't want in our work environment. I can tell you we do *not* want an employee who talks and jokes about "shutting the Lieutenant Commander up—"

Jalen could not remember the last time someone had interrupted him. It had been so long that he could not remember for a second how to react.

"Hey, I thought you had left, Sir. I wouldn't have said that if I had stopped to make sure you had left. My bad."

"That's your comeback?" Jalen wondered if he was about to throw a woman out of the warehouse for the first time.

Finally Len found his opportunity to jump in. "What the hell is going on here, Jalen? Is this some sort of a joke? You're feeling a need to set me up with a woman? *This woman?*"

"Hold on, cowboy," Bonde said. "No one is setting anybody up with anyone. Not in the way I figure you're implying. I don't need anyone to set me up on a date, so get over yourselves. And, Jalen, before you fire me, let me make it easy for you. I thought I would be interested in your job vacancy, but I was wrong. I wouldn't work here for double the salary you offered. I'll show myself out."

Bonde wasn't sure her last comment was a smart one. She left in a huff, hoping she had turned in the right direction.

"For God sake, Len," Jalen said, "help me out here. She's going to get herself lost looking for the exit. Round her up and have a talk with her. Maybe she's having a bad day. I would like us to salvage this if we can. Hawaii 5.0 would not have recommended her to us if they weren't 100% sure that she was qualified for the job. What do you think?"

"Jalen, Bonde and I were passengers on the flight from Toronto to Hawaii. She was following me...no doubt in my mind. She tried to hit on me in the airport lounge! What was that all about? And now she shows up here looking for work! Where did you find her?"

Len was on high alert and Jalen could see it. He didn't want Len to take a swing at him so he tried to settle down before he spoke and hoped Len would do the same. "Len, I didn't *find* Bonde. 5.0 called me and asked if we had any openings and if so they felt they had the ideal candidate. Try to remember Len that 5.0 have their own human resources department, and that's something I like to take advantage of at every opportunity. That's how *you* came to me. I bet you didn't know that."

"No. I didn't."

Jalen hoped Len was settled down enough for the 'ask.' "Can you work with me here, Len?"

Without a second of hesitation Len replied. "When I came to you

I was neither a human nor a resource and I will forever be grateful. Leave Bonde to me... don't rip her papers up just yet."

Carol Ann Cole

28: Cape St. Something

"Did you think we would ever track Lee down? Come on, tell me the truth." Denis was watching his brother carefully.

"I was worried at first," Waine said. "After all, you and I can't claim to be private investigators like Thomas and Paradise. But, by God, we found them. Cape St Something in a province, not a state."

Waine was enjoying this and was very proud of himself. "They have a postal code not a zip code...and of course the biggest difference of all is that Cape St Something has Wikolia's boy and we want him to come home, right?"

"That's absolutely correct. Good research right there!" Denis knew positive reinforcement was necessary for Waine's progress. Many months had passed since the brothers had learned their sister was dead.

Waine had been a mess leading up to and finally confirming their worst fears. Thomas had been trying to find them to tell them their only sister was dead. Waine had spent eight months in the same Mental Health Hospital in Honolulu where Wikolia lived out the end of her young life.

Doctor Legault had assured Denis that, if Waine could make it a positive trip as they sought their nephew, this would be a great aid in his recovery. Waine had responded well to Denis and to the doctors.

Thinking back to their conversations once they returned to their own little piece of Hawaii, Denis could recall every word. Waine hadn't sounded like himself, but at least he was talking back then. Denis knew Waine was heading down a very dark path. He could only hope it wasn't the same path that Wikolia took.

"Where do we start, brother? You tell me. *Tell me,* for Christ's sake, Denis. My sister is dead."

"She's also my sister, Waine."

"I know. I can't think straight. Tell me again what Doctor Legault told us. I know she's dead and gone but what else?"

"She was pregnant and the father of her baby was *not* Thomas."

"That's right. See, I forgot that. That's what I mean about my mind. Something is wrong with me."

"As of this moment, you and I are officially retired. We aren't going to call ourselves Cage Fighters any longer. We boxed for how many years before we switched to Fight Club? That makes us old. We are retired boxers and that's no lie. Got it?"

"I like it," Waine said. "*Retired boxers* it is. Thanks, Denis. You think of everything. Thanks for sticking by me through this long hospital stay. I appreciate you. I need to find something to do that improves my mind, too."

Denis and Waine had left the hospital that day with Doctor Legault walking them to their car. He had spoken quietly to Denis and suggested he 'keep an eye on his brother' and to call if they needed help.

Denis had not shared that detail with his brother. He hoped it wouldn't come to that, but he would keep Doctor Legault's business card with him at all times, just in case.

The brothers drove home in silence, grabbed a couple cans of beer and sat at opposite ends of the kitchen table. It wasn't that they wanted to sit far apart but they always wanted to look at each other and had done so for years.

"Do you think I'm all better now?" Waine still seemed child-like when he spoke.

"Well, no, I don't think you're 'all' better, Waine. You've worked hard, though, and it's paying off. That's why Doctor Legault agreed I could take you on a road trip to find, and get to know, our nephew. We will continue with your therapy every day. The good doctor has taught me well."

"I'll be the judge of that," Waine said with a tiny smile.

"That's what I've been missing. Your smile is a gift, and I'll take it,"

Denis hauled a much-folded wad of papers out of his back pocket. "I've got our trip all planned just they way we like everything to be. Do you want to hear about our trek to Cape St Mary? That's the name of the village where Lee lives: Cape St Mary."

Denis looked up from his notes to see that Waine's eyes were closing. He was sitting upright, hands on his knees, looking straight ahead, yet he was nodding off.

Denis put the notes away, for now. "Come on, tired old man. I've pulled the blankets off the bed just the way you like it. Right to the bottom of the bed. So let's get you in there."

"Sorry, Denis. I do want to hear about our trip but is it okay if I go to sleep? We can review that stuff in the morning."

"That's exactly what we'll do. I'm going to set the table for breakfast and I'll lay the maps out and our tickets and our spending money all out for you to see. If you get up before me you can check it all out then ask me anything you want when I get up."

"You're the best brother in the world, Denis. I love you. Good night."

"Sleep tight, buddy."

Before going to bed himself, Denis made sure his brother would see exactly what he had been told he would see when he walked into the kitchen in the morning. The boys always carried money belts, and the cash sat divided by two in the middle of the table. Given their size they never worried about being robbed...hadn't happened yet.

Beside the cash, Waine would see the airline tickets. Their first flight from Honolulu to Toronto, Canada was a long one and Denis had some concerns about Waine's mental health at the end of that trip.

They would stay in Toronto for two nights and a therapist would come directly to their hotel room if they needed one. Doctor Legault had called on his father, a retired therapist who would be staying in the same hotel as the boys, so if he was needed he would be right there. If he wasn't needed, he and his wife would have a mini vacation before returning to their little house in Pickering.

They hardly ever ventured into the city itself, so this would be an escape from the normal, an overnight mini-vacation. And, at their son's expense!

Sleep escaped Denis. He sat on the side of his bed, reliving all the memories he and Waine had made together. Family memories, of course, but business memories, too. Fighting had been their business. Taking each other on at the Fight Club and being the last *two* men standing in the Cage Finale wasn't all that long ago, so what the Hell happened to his brother? His hulking brother now needed help saying what he wanted to say, help with dressing, eating and even turning on the television, for God's sake.

Grabbing a notepad and pen from the table beside his bed, Denis wrote carefully, speaking each word as he scratched it into the page. "Call Doctor about his father, retired Doctor J. C. Legault, to see if perhaps they would like an all expense paid trip to Nova Scotia in Canada." Denis figured he could make the call from the Honolulu airport as they waited for their flight.

29: From *that* girl

"Hey Pops, what a nice surprise," Paradise said. "You didn't plan another of your infamous homecoming parties for us, did you? We were just up to Halifax."

"I know."

Isn't it kind of late for you to be out?"

Thomas sat their backpacks by the door. He wasn't sure Paradise had seen Eugenie sleeping soundly on the sofa in the family room. "Not too late when you bring your wife along, right Pops? How are you doing, old man?"

"Please, just sit down, you two. Both kids are fast asleep and I have been pacing the floor, wondering if I've done the right thing. My mind is going a thousand miles an hour and my head feels about to explode."

Pops reached into his pants pocket and pulled out the letter. *The letter.* The one that wasn't addressed to him but he took anyway because he wanted Paradise home and in the house before Hope opened it.

"What is it, Pops? Is that for me or for Thomas perhaps?"

"It's for Hope. At least, it's addressed to Hope. It's from that girl I told you I don't like. I think she's a bad influence on Hope. I realize Hope doesn't need a third parent, but I'm worried about all of this. This girl is still pestering her and now she's trying to reach her by mail rather than by phone. That's because you told her not to call here again."

"Who are you talking about, Pops?" Thomas said. "What do you mean when you say you wonder if you've done the right thing?"

Passing the envelope to Thomas, Pops mumbled, "She calls herself Francis with-an-i." You could hear the worry in his voice.

Thomas passed the envelope to Paradise. She would know what to do. Pops sat down and motioned for Thomas to sit beside him. He had already decided to let Eugenie sleep so he didn't need a seat for her.

Paradise was suddenly in tears. "This woman is dangerous and I have no problem telling Hope I have opened this envelope."

"Sweetheart," Thomas said, "I'm just wondering if it would be better to have Hope open it in front of us? It is addressed to her."

"I'll take my chances with Hope. She will understand." Paradise tore the envelope open as she spoke.

Thomas watched closely as she extracted the contents and scanned them. "It's a personal letter, as we would expect from this person."

Paradise looked up at Thomas and Pops before continuing to read in silence.

Pops shifted uneasily. "What does it say? I hope I didn't do the wrong thing."

"Don't say that again, Pops." Paradise snapped. Then she looked up. "Oh, I am sorry. Please...just wait a second while I take this in."

They barely dared breathe as Paradise read and re-read. Finally she looked up, pale-faced. "Dear God, it's a suicide note and the person she wrote her final letter to is *our* daughter."

"It's late," said Pops, "I'm going to wake my bride up and take her home. She hasn't been feeling all that good so I wanted to let her sleep. Oh, and she knows nothing about Francis with-an-i and if it's okay with both of you I would like to keep it that way, at least for now. I don't think we need to talk about this again immediately."

"The hour is very late, and we all need to sleep on this," Paradise said. "And yes, we need not speak of this immediately. I'm not sure yet how to handle this with Hope, but I will give her the letter when the time is right. It's addressed to her."

Thomas walked Pops and Eugenie to the door. He murmured, "Pops, you did the right thing. You're a very kind and caring man and we appreciate you."

"Thank you for saying that, Thomas. I didn't think I would be able to sleep tonight, but you've made it easier. My heart is not as heavy now."

Pops took his bride's hand and lead her home.

30: Feeling some sad

As soon as Eugenie and Pops were out the door and away from the house floodlights, Eugenie made a point of snapping her hand away from her husband's.

Not realizing her action was intentional, Pops reached for her hand a second time. "Give me your hand, my love. You sure didn't look well tonight. Are you feeling okay?"

"Judging by what I heard you say, while you thought I was napping back there, it seems you had already made the decision that I was unwell."

"What? Wait...why were you pretending to be sleeping if you were awake and eavesdropping on me?"

"Eavesdropping on you, Pops? *Really?* I thought we went to the big house simply to be around after Hope and Sky went to bed and to wait until Paradise and Thomas got home. Did I have that wrong?"

Pops began to speak and 'the hand' appeared in his face. He knew better than to interrupt his wife when she was talking. 'On a roll' would be more like it, but he would keep that to himself.

"When did you become a PI? Why didn't I know you had taken an envelope that was meant for someone else and then, of all things, give it to that poor girl's mother? How dare you, Pops? How would you feel if someone took mail that was meant for *you* and gave it to someone else because they didn't think you should have it even though your damn name was on the envelope?"

"Language, as Paradise would say." Pops was hoping for a smile if nothing else. It was as if he hadn't said a word. No acknowledgement at all. Eugenie's rant was far from over and Pops considered telling her to shut up. He didn't, of course!

"I am going to speak my mind and then you are going to get some bedding out of the closet and sleep on the sofa. While you're there, you can think about how you made me feel tonight. First of all you kept me completely out of the loop. You told me nothing about your plan. I wonder if that was because you knew I would not agree with you. Hope is going to be so angry with you, Pops, and you deserve that. Remember when you were a kid and how important your privacy was? You invaded that young woman's privacy in her own home." Eugenie knew she was finding different words to say the same thing and she also knew that she had blown the whole thing way out of proportion.

"You really expect me to sleep on that tiny sofa in the front room? Eugenie, we haven't slept apart since our wedding day. Please tell me I don't really have to sleep on that sofa. I'll break my back on that thing."

"I'll tell you what we are going to do. We are going to get ready for bed then come back downstairs and have a nightcap sitting right here. While we enjoy our drink you can *attempt* to help me see that what you did was not wrong. Oh, and don't get me started on how angry you made me with your little, 'Eugenie hasn't been feeling well. I'm going to let her sleep.' You should have added, 'I want to tell you about this letter behind my wife's back,' then they would have had the whole picture."

"I'm rethinking that drink, my darling wife. The sofa is going to be just fine for me. You go off and enjoy our bed. Maybe you'll be in a better mood in the morning. I'll have coffee ready whenever you want it, but please don't bring your bad attitude down those stairs when you join me."

"Please, Pops, have a night-cap with me. Help me understand why that letter was so important to you in the first place."

"No! I'll just get my bedding and I'll be out of your way. I don't really feel like talking anymore tonight. I need to walk away from this conversation, Eugenie. I'm feeling some sad, I will admit. Good night."

Eugenie remained motionless until Pops returned with his bedding. "So you found everything you need then? I wasn't sure you even knew where we keep it."

Now it was her turn to have an attempt to make the other person smile fall flat.

She watched as Pops put the bedding down and came back to her. She wasn't sure she had ever felt such relief when he sat down again.

Short-lived relief. Because then he told her about the letter, as much as he knew about this Francis-with-an-i, and what Paradise had said was in it. "I think she was trying to have a relationship with Hope and was becoming more and more forceful. Any of this ringing a bell?"

Pops stopped because Eugenie was crying and he hated to be the cause of her shedding even one tear.

Eugenie was heartbroken, but she understood everything now. Best to sleep on it so she took herself to bed.

She missed her husband the second she pulled the covers up over her in their bed. *My own damn fault,* she reminded herself before drifting off.

Carol Ann Cole

31: Hot tongue and cold shoulder

Pops was some mad. "Damn sofa is meant for sitting, not sleeping. I feel like Hell this morning and I'm still not sure I did anything wrong."

Pops was multitasking, as the smart business folks in the Cape were all bragging about, doin' a million things at once. *I'll settle for doing two things at once*, he decided.

Pops was making coffee and he was having a rather loud discussion with himself. The coffee was hot and, given that he had been up for over an hour, he wanted his wife up with him. He was planning to say he didn't think he was talking that loud if he felt he needed to defend his actions to Eugenie.

Maybe he wasn't making enough noise...but then she let him know she was up with a slamming of either their bedroom or bathroom door.

Pops had turned his chair so his only view was through the kitchen window where he could watch the locals rush by early in the morning. He didn't want to be the first to speak when Eugenie made her appearance, so this way he could ignore her for a bit longer.

He hoped she was in a better mood than he was. Maybe getting married at his age had been a mistake? Pops was aware he might be overreacting.

Eugenie had heard her husband very clearly, as he scraped the coffee pot across the kitchen counter and then began his all-too-loud and one-sided conversation. She went into the bathroom and slammed the door to give her husband a warning that she was getting up and could hear his angry voice. Sleep had been sporadic for Eugene and she imagined it had been worse for Pops.

114

Pops heard her coming down the hall and into the kitchen. He took a loud noisy sip of hot coffee just in case she hadn't seen him over by the window.

Eugenie poured herself a cup of coffee and brought the pot with her as she placed her mug on the table beside Pops. "Good morning...can I top up your coffee for you?"

"I'm good for now. I've been up for ages."

"Yes, I know exactly when you got up from the sofa, folded the bedding, brought it into the bedroom and put it away, making more noise than bedding should make. I heard you drag the coffee pot out too...but none of that matters. As the kids say, 'May I please have a do-over for last evening?' Is that possible?"

She sat down beside him, pulled the curtain back a bit more so she too could see out the window. If Pops wanted silence she could give him that...all day long. He'd better be careful.

"I'm too old to waste time fighting with you, Eugenie. I'm sorry I didn't include you in my worries about the letter. And I'm sorry I didn't apologize last night so we could go to bed together. And if there is anything else I should apologize for, consider it done."

"Was it a conscious decision to exclude me? It just doesn't seem like you would do such a thing, Pops. We talk about everything. We keep no secrets and we don't play games, right?"

"I didn't hear much of what you just said because I don't get why you're asking if I was conscious or not. Of-bloody-course I was conscious, so please don't make me feel stupid about all of this. I don't get it!"

Pops got up to pour another cup of coffee and took his time sitting back down.

Eugenie wanted to ask if it had been a conscious decision to not offer her a refill as she had done when she poured her first cup, but she figured that would add to his confusion. She found his interpretation of 'conscious decision' very sweet.

She knew about all the years Paradise helped Pops with his words and all the hours he had spent doing his homework right beside Hope as she worked on hers. Eugenie decided to keep this *teachable moment* for another time.

"I shouldn't have used that expression, and I'm sorry I did, Pops. Let's talk about something else...in the name of the Lord, let's talk about something else."

Eugenie knew that would make Pops laugh and they hadn't laughed together for almost twenty-four hours. There was absolutely no need for that. They had both behaved like children... badly-behaved children.

"Saved by the doorbell," Pops said as he rushed to open the door. He was surprised when he saw who it was.

32: Take my clothes off?

"Good morning to you young lady. What on earth are you doing knocking on our door before school?" Pops hugged Hope and she hugged him back. Hugging was their thing, as they told anyone who asked either of them why they hug so much. Love and respect for each other was how Pops liked to explain it.

"Can I at least come inside before I tell you why I'm here?" Hope pointed to the raindrops forming on her shoulders.

"Of course. Come in, my dear. You're not sick, are you? You're not skipping school, I hope?"

"Pops, let Hope come in and sit down. What can I get you, dear?" Eugenie loved Hope and the feeling was mutual.

"I just wanted to say something to both of you. It's about Francis with-an-i. Pops, my mom told me about you kind of playing detective and removing the letter that was clearly addressed to me. Am I right so far?"

"You are correct, Hope, and that was all my fault. Eugenie would know better than to do something stupid like that."

Taking his hand, Eugenie said, "That's not necessary to say, Pops. You thought you were doing the right thing. I understand that now." Watching Pops reach out and hug Eugenie made Hope smile.

"Hey, hey, can we get back to *me* here? This is all about me at the moment, if you don't mind."

Hope paused to make sure they both knew she was joking. "I want to do the talking and I do have to go to school, as you so correctly pointed out, Pops. As the song says, 'times a wastin', so may I continue?"

Pops could see that Hope didn't seem to be mad at him so he

was feeling a bit better than he had when she first began talking about Francis with-an-i.

"I'm not mad or anything, so I'll say that first because you both seem a bit wary about why I'm really here. I came to thank you, Pops, for having obviously been so aware when she was at my house or when she called me on the phone...every damn day. At first I was kind of flattered that an old woman, well you both know what I mean when I say an *old woman*, like Francis with-an-i would want to spend any time with me. But...when I understood that she wanted me to *take my clothes off* I just wanted to go home and tell my mother."

Hope paused for a second because she could see both Pops and Eugenie had been shocked when she got to the 'take my clothes off' part of her story.

Eugenie reached over to take Hope's hand. "Oh, my land, girl, are you okay? Did that monster touch you?"

"No, no, I got out of there with my clothes on, and then I asked mom to make sure Francis with-an-I didn't bother me. I didn't ask for her help right away, but I was worried about it. I told mom everything on our way to Honolulu to help Thomas after Wikolia died. We talked about it again on the flight back to Toronto. Mom even talked to *her* on the phone and then mom and dad went to see my principal at school. He had already fired her, though. I'm thinking this is more details than you need, but it's all part of why I am here to thank you, Pops, for giving that letter to my mother."

Hope reached for the apple juice Eugenie had poured for her.

"Hope, did the school principal fire her because she was...you know...because she liked girls?" Pops turned to Eugenie and said, "That might have been too personal a question, I guess. Sorry, ladies."

"Would she be what they call a queer, or is there something worse than that?" Eugenie was intrigued with the discussion and wanted to learn more. "Is that even allowed? I thought it was illegal."

"Ah...I think you've said enough," Pops said.

"Don't gang up on me, you two," Eugenie responded. "Living in a convent from just about your age, Hope, until I turned 21, I can tell you that this has been a rather informative morning so far. Hope, I want you to know that Pops and I are so proud of you and so happy you feel comfortable sharing all of that...sex talk with us."

"Thunderin' Jesus, woman, Hope did *not* mention sex." Pops wouldn't admit it, but because of the bond he shared with Hope he was enjoying the discussion as well. Hope was comfortable coming to them with this personal story ...and he was thankful.

Hope was laughing as she watched the bride and groom, as so many in the Cape called them, talk back and forth with such excite‐ment. "Okay, I need to get to the important part in the letter, be‐cause mom will soon be here to pick me up for school. For sure my mother will think I should have been through talking *long* before now."

Hesitating for no more than a few seconds, Hope reached into her pocket and pulled the letter out. "I'll leave this so you can read it on your own. I really would appreciate it if you both read it be‐cause I am so shocked by this I might need to talk about it for the next ten years!"

"Is it all about sex dear and what Francis with-an-i wants you to do with her when she gets your clothes off?" Before she could con‐tinue, Eugenie put her hands over her mouth.

"You better keep your hands over your mouth, woman. Let's let the girl tell us about the contents of the letter rather than guess what this damn piece of paper is all about. I wish our mailman had lost it or thrown it out by mistake."

33: Confirmation of suicide

"It's all okay, Pops," Hope said. "I don't mind the questions, but no, the letter is not about anything like that, Eugenie. It's the most terrible thing..."

Hope reached for her glass of apple juice again because she was about to cry and she had promised herself she would not do that. Pops hated to see her cry and she didn't like to put him in that position. It made him uncomfortable and he had had enough sad in his life. Putting her glass down she was pretty sure she could get through this without any tears.

"Take your time, love." Pops reached over and rubbed her shoulder.

"It was, or I guess it is, a suicide letter. Francis with-an-i wrote that she was going to kill herself. Isn't that the most awful thing ever? Imagine finding yourself in a place where you saw suicide as being your best choice. Or maybe, you felt suicide was your only choice, so..."

"Sorry to interrupt, dear," Eugenie said.

She stood up, approached Hope and encouraged her to stand up as well. "Pops, follow us. Kitchen chairs, and kitchens in general, are not meant for such terrible news. We can continue in our front room. Hope, why don't you sit right here between us." Eugenie patted the sofa between Pops and herself and encouraged Hope to sit there.

"We have to watch the clock," Hope said. "Mom is driving me to school so she can show this letter to the principal. I'm going to the office with her. Mom says none of this is my fault but I'm not convinced that's true."

Hope held up her hands as both Pops and Eugenie tried to inter-

rupt. "We think Francis with-an-i mailed this letter just before doing it...the suicide thing, I mean."

Hope began to cry as her mother walked in. She had been okay
emotionally but she knew with her mom in the room she could
crash for a minute or two. She needed a good cry and another glass
of apple juice.

"Tough morning for my girl today. Hope, honey, let's hustle off to
your school and to the principal's office. He will be shocked when
he reads this letter. He might be able to tell us if he has heard anything about Francis with-an-I since she left the school. An obituary
or something similar." Paradise showed no emotion. In the moment, she was a momma-bear protecting her child.

Pops stood and gathered Hope into his arms. "Honey, this is
something I would normally seek permission for from your mom,
but I bet if you asked your mom she would let you come home with
her and play hooky for the rest of the day. I think this would be a
perfect day for you and me to take my boat out or just go down the
wharf and sit in it as we have done so many times."

Eugenie interrupted. "I love that idea and I would go with you
and Pops but need to remind you that I have a tendency to throw
up when I'm out on the ocean. Pops learned that the hard way." Eugenie knew her comment would change the mood and she was
right.

"We needed that, Eugenie," Paradise said. "Thanks for letting us
all share a laugh. I love your idea of Hope coming back home with
me rather than spending the rest of the day in class, but I don't
know. She might not want to take the day off."

After thanking and hugging both Pops and Eugenie, Paradise
ushered her daughter out the door and to the car.

Hope looked back before getting in and said, "I won't be long,
Pops. I'll come and pick you up so we can walk over to your boat
together, okay?"

Before Pops could speak, Eugenie offered her own idea. "Why
don't I make up a nice lunch for you two? Since it's already been a
tough day I promise it will be an extra special lunch. Now get going."

34: Bonde and her boy

"Don't argue with me." Bonde was enjoying this as she moved closer. "Look at you, for Christ's sake. You're still wet behind the ears. We've been on the night shift for how many days?" Pause for response. None offered.

"Oh, handsome. I've got you all figured out." Bonde ran her fingers over Lenny's face and then walked out of his room. She knew he was looking at her ass.

Lenny was deep in thought. *If the truth were to come out that the new recruit, who happens to be female, makes me nervous I'll never hear the end of it.*

Bonde had immediately, on day one, made sure to call him Lenny around anyone who would listen. So, once again he was Lenny and not Len. Lieutenant Commander Jalen Lexis would not be pleased. At the very least, Jalen would not want details.

One thing Lenny would *never* do, *never* in a million years, was date the woman who replaced the woman who stole his heart. "Someone told me to never say never, but in this case it's a must." Lenny was officially talking to himself.

Lenny was convinced he had loved Paradise from the second he met her. He knew even back then that she had a partner. She lived with Thomas Adams. He knew they weren't married, though. When he thought the time was right, he had quit his job and followed her from Honolulu to a tiny village in Nova Scotia, up in Canada. Some would call that stalking and Lenny knew it.

But it didn't matter what anyone called it. Lenny learned Paradise was not in love with him.

Lenny had worked with Paradise on the night shift, and now on the same shift Bonde was the new Paradise. Who would have guessed *that* might happen!

Because Lenny never left the warehouse, the night shift would always be his best option. His 24-hour confinement on the inside was an almost-certain guarantee that he would not be killed. Lenny was convinced that if he left the premises he would be shot dead before he could reach his car.

"Hey there, boy, why don't you lend me your car?" Bonde had asked. "You're on the inside until Witness Protection comes calling, right? I promise to keep her, assuming your car is a she, purring exactly the way you will have me purring the minute you insert your key into me. Is that too nasty for your virgin ears, Lenny?"

Bonde was enjoying this, way too much, and she couldn't stop smiling at her boy.

"Listen to me. My car will just disappear one day. I don't want the stress of you being taken and possibly hurt because I had loaned it to you."

Lenny's story had made her laugh at him and he didn't like that. Much of his youth had been spent hiding from his father or having his peers at school laugh at him. He was never sure why he was the butt of so many jokes. Maybe Bonde saw in him the same things that the bullies at school saw. She had a way of knocking the confidence out of Lenny every time they were together, and that was every single day.

Shortly after the 'car' discussion with Bonde, Lenny had asked Jalen to take the car back, since he would not be driving it. He further asked that that happen while he and Bonde were working. He didn't want any chance of her seeing Jalen driving his car. "It's complicated, Jalen..."

"In the name of God, why does everyone want to tell me more than I need to know? If it's complicated it's not a stretch to assume emotions are involved and emotions are above my pay grade. As far as the car goes, consider it done."

"I appreciate that—"

"I wasn't finished, *Lenny*," Jalen said. "If you have some romantic notion about Bonde, if you are going down the same damn road you travelled with Paradise, leave me out of it."

"Not going to happen, boss."

Jalen wasn't sure he believed that. He had seen the way Bonde acted around Lenny. Few single men can stay away from a woman like Bonde if she constantly tried to get their attention. Especially at the end of a long shift. Lenny had discussed his possibility of re-joining the Witness Protection Program (WPP) with Jalen and then with 'the team' that would direct his application going forward with zero involvement from anyone at 2.0. It was pretty much the same drill, but given that Lenny had turned this down just seconds before it was to take effect the first time, there wasn't a lot of support to move his application forward any time soon. He knew this; he understood, and that was on him.

Living on the outside, so to speak, Bonde was enjoying her job and she was enjoying her workmate even more. Surprised to see how genuinely shy Lenny was, she was prepared to take things slow. That was a first for Bonde.

She always found a reason to go to Lenny's bunkhouse at the end of shift. Her greatest hope was that one day she would catch him already in bed and stark naked under the sheets. Hadn't happened yet...Lenny had caught on to what she was doing, and was prepared to sleep in his clothes all night long to ensure she didn't catch him naked. She wasn't about to give up trying, though.

Bonde wasn't used to working the night shift, and being off all day, every day offered a learning curve for her. She didn't need much sleep, but she did need whatever hours she was to sleep to be at night, not when the sun was shining and her surfing buddies wanted her riding the waves with them, not at home in bed.

When Lieutenant Commander Jalen Lexis first met with Bonde, he gave her some background on how and why the night shift work plan had evolved.

Initially 2.0 hired a private investigator by the name of Thomas Adams to fill the night shift role. Who he brought on as part of his team was up to him. Paradise...he brought his life and work partner, Paradise.

Initially she and Lenny were to sleep on site and really just listen to ensure no one broke into the warehouse. They were 2.0's living insurance plan. It was less expensive to pay the salaries of two employees than have their overall insurance policies cover the warehouse when it was empty. The only difference was that Paradise would go home during the day and Lenny would not. His home was on the inside...at the 2.0 warehouse.

Over time, Paradise and Lenny did a bit of work together at the beginning of shift and again around 6:30 am. They were both up very early and in need of a coffee. They soon learned they worked well together and the night shift provided more productive hours once they found a balance.

Thomas had become a single parent when Paradise took her two-month vacation with Hope. It looked like a short-term assignment, just replacing Paradise until the fall, so Thomas slept at the warehouse every night and went home to his son and to the hospital where Wikolia had lived during the day.

This went on to be a long-term assignment for Thomas, but the money was good and he needed the cash. He was responsible for additional expenses, like his son's nanny and the medical expenses for Wikolia that his insurance policy didn't cover.

35: Adoption!

"Wilmot, my love, do you ever get tired of our routine life? How we have everything planned and we rarely deviate from the plan?"

Marie had wanted to bring this up for some time and she decided it was time. They were about half way through their early morning walk along Mavillette Beach. She had stopped and stood facing her husband holding both of his hands to keep him close.

"Why do I feel blindsided by this, Marie? My God, how long have you been so unhappy?" Wilmot was almost in tears and clearly shocked by his wife's admission of being so unhappy with their life.

He could see that she was trying to respond to his questions so he squeezed both of her hands and nodded at her to continue to explain. He fought his inner demons because what he really wanted to do in the moment was race back to their cottage and bury his head under a pillow. "I'm making a mess of this, Wilmot, so let me start again."

"Talk to me, please. And let's keep walking. I need my 'routine,' as you call it. I'll shut up now." Wilmot was shaking.

Marie decided to begin at the end. Wilmot had completely misunderstood her silly questions and she needed to help him calm down...immediately. "*A dog!* A rescue dog. I want to talk to you about the possibility of us adopting a rescue dog, Wilmot. That's what I'm trying to say. I apologize for not saying it properly. Some days I still struggle with my mental health and my words, as you know."

Wilmot peered intently at her. Then a slow smile spread across his face. "Can we call our dog 'Rescue'?"

He gave her hand a tug and they started walking back toward

their cottage. "I almost had a heart attack when you started asking me personal questions. I was about to ask you to call for help."

Finally Wilmot was able to smile. He, too, had mental heath issues and he tried to not over-react. Together they were works in progress and they worked on their mental health each and every day. "Rescue is a great name," Marie said as they reached their cottage and opened the door. "Does this mean you won't mind sharing me with another?"

She was laughing now and Wilmot could see that this possibility of finding a dog was both a great idea and a morale booster. "Come on, sweetheart, let's shower then find out where the closest rescue dog place is."

Later, as they drove away from Cape St Mary toward Yarmouth, where they believed they would find a dog shelter, Marie was working on a list of what they would need to purchase after buying the dog. They weren't even sure if they had to pay anything for a rescue dog. Maybe there would be no charge?

They had money with them and they had the location of a dog shelter. They would purchase a bed, a food dish, a water dish, dog food and maybe a few doggie toys. Marie often saw dog owners give their dog a 'treat' for doing something well, so she added dog treats to her list. But she put a question mark at the end because she wasn't at all familiar with what dog treats might be.

Then she laughed out loud. "I forgot to put 'dog' first on my list, Wilmot! No need for anything else on my list if we don't find Rescue."

Wilmot, eyes on the road, reached out and took her hand.

"List complete," Marie said. "So now let's talk about how Rescue will change our lives. I was going to make another list, but I realize you're driving in silence even though I'm sitting right here. Sorry about that, honey. I'm all yours, so do you want to start? Tell me why you agreed to finding a dog so quickly and how you feel our lives will change."

"The good news," Wilmot began, "is that we already take two rather long walks a day. I think adding a dog to our routine is a great idea. And if we have to add a third or forth walk, we will do that, too. I hope we will be able to leave Rescue at home when we go for groceries, for appointments and for church, but other than that I think we will bring him or her with us. Do you agree with that, Marie?"

"Oh, yes I do! Imagine how a dog would love to roll around on Mavillette beach and in the water when we are walking there morning and night—"

"This is reminding me to hurry up and install that outside tap. I will pick up a hose while we're in town. Rescue will need to be washed to rid him or her of the salt water and sand before putting a paw inside of our home."

"Got it. I just added 'hose' to our list. Do you care what kind of dog, or what gender, we get? I don't have any preference at all. I guess a rescue shelter has a bit of everything so I think we are meant to pick a dog that needs our help just as we needed help all those years ago when we were both beaten and left for dead. I sort of feel this is our own small way of giving back to humanity. Is that too much of a stretch?"

"Not at all. Marie, I continue to marvel at your ability to see the positive in everything. I hadn't thought about this being a way to give back to our community, but you're right...it really is."

They drove around downtown Yarmouth to look for the shelter they had read about in their local flyer. "The ad was lovely. I really do have a good feeling about our day." Marie was very happy.

"There it is, Marie. Just up the street on the left. And, here's a place to park right in front of the store."

"Oh, Wilmot, look at that sweet dog. How much is that doggie in the window? That's the one I want."

"Let's go inside before we make our decision."

Wilmot opened the door and stepped aside with a big grin on his face. He made sure Marie was safely inside before following her into the shelter.

He had a good feeling about their decision.

36: Rescuee to the rescue

"Oh, Wilmot, if this isn't our Rescuee, I'll just die. Isn't she perfect? I had no idea you can just walk into a shelter and pick a dog and take her home with you. How easy is this going to be? I love it here, Wilmot, do you?"

Wilmot loved the way Marie seemed to fall for every dog she looked at. "Let's not get ahead of ourselves, now. There are rows and rows of kennels to check out. They look like ordinary crates, to be honest, so let's get one special dog out of a crate and on to Mavillette Beach. That will be heaven for our puppy."

Wilmot was just as happy about this as Marie. Something positive for them to carve out and make their own…a family with their dog.

Seeing how happy the couple appeared to be, the owner of the Animal Shelter spoke up over the continuous barking. "Welcome, and thank you for stopping by. My name is Karen. Some of the dogs will cower in the corner of their cage, because they are scared when they see a new human. See how their ears are flattened back to their heads? They are afraid of strangers. Most of our dogs have trust issues. That's part of what makes them a 'rescue.' I'll leave you to visit with the dogs. You can bring your questions and your personal choices to me anytime you're ready."

"Oh, thank you so much," Marie said. "I'm in love with all of them, which is what my husband was afraid of."

She turned to locate Wilmot, and saw him sitting on the floor in front of a kennel, which brought him to eye level with whatever was inside it. She turned back to Karen. "You'll have to excuse me. It looks like my husband might have found our dog!"

Wilmot, without turning his head, raised his hand to signal her to join him. When she drew close, he spoke in a low, even voice. "This little puppy is the only one not barking. Look how she is sitting with her ears up as if to say, 'pick me, pick me.' She's posing, I think. Watch her turn her head from side to side. It sure looks like she's posing to me."

"I can bring that one out to visit with you, if you like," Karen said.

"Oh, yes," Marie said.

Karen stepped forward. "Let me put a leash on her. And when I let her out, please be ready for a full-on performance. This lady is delightful."

The dog stole the show. She danced around and around chasing her tail, something she could not do in the crate. She jumped higher and then higher than the last time, while watching Wilmot and Marie for their reaction.

"Come here, girl," Marie said as she reached out to pet the 'performer.' "I think we will take you home with us. Did you know your name is Rescuee? I picked your name out myself. Now, let's go and talk with daddy. I'll do the talking, if that's okay with you, girl. Come with me."

Marie took the leash from Karen's hand and walked over to where Wilmot was sitting. But she didn't get a chance to speak, Rescuee said it all by wedging herself between her new mommy and daddy with her nose firmly planted under their interlocked hands. She licked one hand and then the other.

Wilmot was the first to speak. He had trouble keeping his emotions in check but managed to say, "I think she picked us, not the other way around. Is this Rescuee, Marie?"

"Yes this is Rescuee, but…" Marie lowered her voice to continue, "I think we should find out how much she costs first. We have a budget, remember."

Still smiling, Wilmot said, "Karen, we'll take her. What do we owe you and can you give us a bit of health history, and what we should expect going forward?"

Before Karen could respond, Marie said, "Her name is Rescuee. Without going into detail, many years ago both my husband and I were rescued from a terrible situation, so we thought we would rescue a dog today."

She turned to the dog. "Do you like your new name?"

Both Marie and Wilmot were looking directly at Rescuee. While one rubbed her belly the other let her lick both hands.

Karen was smiling broadly. "Rescuee was dropped off one morning before we were even here to open the door and turn the lights on. She was in pretty bad shape and appeared nearly starved to death. This happens more than the public may realize, which is why I'm so happy to see her bonding with you. I do want to be honest with you about her health issues though."

"It sounds as if Rescuee's past is somewhat similar to ours," Wilmot said, "so I would like to think she will understand us and know right away...right now in fact...that we are here for her and we will—"

"And we love her," Marie said. She sat on the floor and began telling her new dog just how lucky she was to be moving to Cape St Mary and Mavillette beach. "We're bringing you with us while we find you a new bed, food and lots and lots of toys. How does that sound?"

"Just to be sure you know everything that you should know," Karen said, "let me tell you we were unable to obtain any past history for Rescuee. We treated her assuming that she had not received the required injections. All of her injections are now up to date. We believe she is a mutt, some combination of breeds."

"A gorgeous mutt," Marie said.

"Additionally, Rescuee seems to have some anxiety issues. She doesn't do well when left alone and she gets very nervous if she is around too many strangers. She doesn't make friends easily...with the exception of the two of you, apparently. Please monitor her health and you will be able to build your own file relative to her health from today going forward."

"All that is good to know," Wilmot said as he got to his feet.

"Please call if you have any questions. Here is my card. We always love to hear how our 'students' are doing after they leave us."

"Now," Wilmot said as he brought out his wallet," what's the damage?"

"There is no cost for the dog. All we ask is that, if you can, you make a donation to our shelter or to a shelter of your choice. Not today, but in the future perhaps."

Bending down to meet Rescuee's eyes, Karen said, "And you, pretty girl, you bring your mommy and daddy back to see us soon. But right now, today, show them the joy that only *you* can spread."

37: Find the child

Sydney had been careful to not say much to her dear friend, Liz. She wasn't sure Liz believed the report Paradise and Thomas had prepared so Liz could get the accused out of the room she had rented to him. Her very young grandchildren came to her kitchen for cookies every day after school.

Yet, when Liz came to her home not 24 hours after Sydney had called her, she was already doubting the PIs' report. "I simply cannot imagine my brother doing anything so vile. I see him every day. Wouldn't I see something or hear something? Pick up on a strange comment from him when he sits with my grandchildren? I'm not a stupid woman, Sydney."

Sydney had been unable to convince her friend that the accused was in all probability going to be found guilty as charged. Sydney made sure Liz knew how *she* felt. The real question was just hanging out of reach. *Should I share, and if so, when will I share the details of my past history involving this monster?* Did Liz deserve to know?

The question Sydney asked herself was far more personal. 'Do I want Paradise to find my child?' Of course the easy answer was, 'Yes, I do.' In the back of her mind she was certain that before he left for prison this monster would destroy everyone who had ever crossed his path...he would certainly try. She would not be spared.

As she thought it through, she worried that her child, if she were able to find her, would think Sydney had only sought her out because of the trial and had simply been trying to stay ahead of the monster.

Not wanting to think it through to the point she would find fault with any decision she might make, Sydney picked up the phone to call her friend.

"Paradise d'Entremont Private Investigator, how may I help you?" Paradise sat up straight and grabbed pen and paper, not knowing who was on the other end of the phone. Both she and Thomas made sure they kept notes in case they felt the need to discuss calls at day's end.

"Paradise, I don't want to say too much on the phone, and I'm a nervous wreck about this decision I've made, but I want you to find the child."

"I'm on it, Sydney. Leave everything with me and I'll be in touch as soon as I have a lead. Is this time sensitive?"

"Is that a problem?"

"Not a problem, however, I do have to ask because of other work we have. I can put you at the top of the list if you say the word."

There was a pause. Paradise listened. She knew this would be gut-wrenching for Sydney.

"Immediately. I would like you on this case as soon as you possibly can be. I'm anxious about this.

"There will be some travelling so, to cover expenses, I may ask for a retainer, but that's for another day."

Then, because it felt personal, Paradise shed a tear as she added, "I'm proud of you, Sydney."

Sydney hung her head before hearing the kind words shared with a professional who was also a friend.

38: Who's the daddy?

"This place is almost as beautiful as home, Waine. Open your eyes and look out the window, brother. You're missing such beautiful scenery."

Waine had sat quietly, albeit wide awake, through their flight from Toronto to Halifax. However, he followed that up by falling soundly asleep while Denis picked up their car rental and was no help at all as Denis loaded their luggage into the car. He brought Waine with him to the car but Denis could only carry one bag while leading Waine as you might lead a child.

Waine continued to sleep while Denis did all the paperwork and the heavy lifting. They had brought too many gifts for Lee, given the weight of their bags. Denis was smiling though. He had a good feeling about this.

Their plan had been to pick up the rental car and drive directly to Cape St Mary. They had booked a small cottage in the Cape and, while Denis was anxious to see his nephew, he knew he should take Waine to their cottage and let him sleep as long as necessary. Dr. Legault had reminded Denis that much of the medication Waine was taking would make him tired and that whenever he needed a nap Denis was to allow that to happen.

It was a lonely life for Denis, but he had already had a great conversation with God and had promised that if God let his brother recover he would care for him every single day of their lives.

So far, so good.

Russ and Carol quickly checked the brothers into their cottage at the Cape View, gave Denis a key and reminded him a complimentary breakfast would be available in the office area every morning.

"What brings you to Paradise, and where are you and your brother from?"

Russ was just being friendly but Denis thought he meant Paradise the person and was none to happy their privacy had been invaded already. "How would you know we are here to see Paradise and her family? We have tried to keep our trip private and—"

"Hold it, man," Russ said. "I call this place paradise on earth. I assure you, I was not talking about Paradise from 548."

"All is forgiven," Denis said. but now he wanted to know more. "Do you know Paradise and her family?"

"Carol and I know everyone in our little village, and you will, too, if you stay for a couple of weeks."

Denis tried again. "Waine and I are from Hawaii and we are here to surprise Paradise and her family. Her partner's name is Thomas, I believe. And their daughter, Hope, as well?"

"I'll not confirm or deny anything, but I will say they also have a small boy, Lee, and by God that child looks a little bit like you. Is that possible?"

This made Denis squirm and it also made him anxious to visit 548. He couldn't wipe the smile off his face as he literally ran back to their cottage to share the good news with Waine.

Meanwhile, back in the office, Carol joined Russ at the registration desk. "Well, well, well, what have we here?"

She checked the details Denis had given, in particular their departure date. "Don't blow this two-week booking by calling Thomas to tip them off that visitors are in town. I know you're thinking about it"

Putting his hands on Carol's shoulders, Russ turned her around so she was facing the big window. They watched as Denis helped Waine into the car. "Operation Lee is about to take off," Russ said.

"Not sure about the kid's name," Carol said. "Do you think this is the child Thomas had with Wikolia or is it the child Wikolia had with someone else? Paradise and I chat when we meet at the start of our morning run. I don't think I've got the facts quite right about Wikolia's babies, though." Carol suspected Russ was not listening. "What do *you* think, Russ?"

"I think you know much more about all of this than I do. But that Denis might be that boy's father. I guess Lee's father could be the other brother, Waine. I didn't see his face...I tried but he seemed to be sleeping."

Russ saw another guest arriving so he put Denis and Waine's card away for now.

39: Talk to me, girl

"Paradise d'Entremont, Private Investigator, how may I help you?"

"It's been a while." Len couldn't help smiling as he spoke. "Talk to me, girl."

He wondered if she would catch his phrasing. He didn't say 'my' girl, which is what Len had called Paradise as they walked along Mavillette beach all those mornings ago. Back then he had believed she *was* his girl. He had been such a fool to think that, but he was left with beautiful memories, if nothing else, so he wasn't complaining.

It was nothing more than a couple of sound bites but Paradise knew exactly who was on the call. "Lenny, I missed seeing you the day we went to 2.0 to gather our things and say bye to everyone. I hope you know that having you in seclusion during our visit was *not* my idea. I had *no* idea until Jalen told us he had ensured we would not run into you."

"Did you ask for me?"

"I did not."

Paradise thought about explaining that everyone was around her the entire time she and Thomas were at the warehouse that last day, but she knew that everything she might say would sound like a blatant excuse. It all added up to nothing more than Paradise not having the guts to speak up to Thomas and Jalen and insist on seeing Lenny.

"I didn't know you were going to be here, Paradise. All I knew was that you were back with Thomas and I didn't need to hear much else."

"'Lenny, I was not *back* with Thomas because I had never left Thomas. My Lord, we talked about this so many times during our walks along Mavillette beach."

"I heard the words but I didn't want to believe them. When you let me hold your hand I took that as a lifeline. A lifeline that you were offering to me was all I could see. It was all in my own head. I know that now."

Paradise kept checking the front door. She didn't want Thomas to surprise her. "How is it that you're calling me today, Lenny? And before you answer, I will admit I'm grateful for your call. I do want you to know that I have pretty much left the local police team. I just have two cases I am wrapping up here and I will move over to our PIU team that Thomas and I have in place. It was in place in Honolulu as well. Thomas and I will be working our cases on the road as required and from our home office. Just hearing your name sets Thomas off and he then thinks all kinds of things are going on between you and me. So, fair warning, if you call and Thomas answers please just ask for me."

Paradise didn't feel good talking about Thomas behind his back, but Lenny needed to be aware of their situation. There was a 50% chance Thomas would answer the phone and Paradise knew this would generate more discussion on 'all things Lenny' after the call was finished.

"Are you saying he's jealous of me?" Lenny silently admitted he kind of liked the idea of Thomas wondering what kind of a hold he still had on Paradise. Thomas should have his total focus on Paradise, not on him.

"Don't get all puffed up, Lenny. I believe Thomas is a bit jealous of you and me together, but not you specifically. I know his mind goes there sometimes when we are off on our own to walk the length of the beach." Paradise trailed off and her mind was elsewhere for a moment.

"Lenny, why are you calling me now? Why now?"

Paradise paused to look around. Coast was still clear so she went on, in an even lower voice. "How are you doing? Have you fit back into the family and what about the witness protection program? Do you have a new work partner?"

"God, it's good to hear your voice, girl."

There was a long pause, and then Paradise heard Lenny draw a shaky breath. "I placed this call to say good-bye to you. I'm in line for entry into WPP. And, uh, I wanted you to know I have met someone. She replaced you here at 2.0. Make no mistake, she hasn't replaced you in my heart, but I'm trying to tuck all thoughts of you into my memory bank so that I have you with me forever. You're the one who taught me about memory banks and I like the idea."

"Does this woman have a name, Lenny?"

"She does. She has a one-word name...*Bonde*. She's good for me right now. You can't imagine the ribbing I take because I'm dating your replacement. It's all in good fun I believe...at least I hope it is. I have become closer to some of the guys who work the floor and that's because Jalen had me stand up and share where I had gone and how that all worked out for me. I guess baring my soul made me more human to them. I sure wasn't expecting the reaction I got. Christ, they applauded me when I finished speaking Paradise, and a number of them lined up to pat me on the back and wish me well."

They pondered that in silence for a bit, then Lenny continued.

"We are all broken in different ways and after I shared all of my sins, some of the others now feel more comfortable doing the same. Does that make sense, Paradise? I know I'm talking too much. You know I do that when I'm nervous. You always make me nervous. Should I let you go? It's just that if this is the last time I'll ever speak with you I'm not sure—"

Paradise had to cut Lenny off. "Lenny, I want you to believe this...I have been wanting to clear things up with you and for us to be able to have a proper good-bye. I had something much bigger in mind than a phone call. I wanted to fly to Honolulu so you and I could sit down, maybe have a coffee together, talk it all out and then wish each other well and sign off. You just beat me to it."

"Well, isn't that typical of how easy I can mess up? I screw up the possibility of seeing you in person, probably right here in the warehouse. Damn. Any way you could still come here to talk?"

"Be honest, Lenny. You know we have said all that needs to be said."

"I guess, but a man can dream. Before we hang up, can I ask how Hope is, and the little guy as well?"

"Thanks for asking. Both kids love it here and if you think you and I loved Mavillette beach, our son, Lee adores it even more. He would spend every day, all day, on the beach if he could. In fact, one of us must have eyes on Lee all the time because he can slip out of the house and run to the ocean in a second. We're teaching him safety and respect for the water, but he's still very young."

"I did not know you had a son. When did that happen? I missed something, somewhere."

"No, Lee is the little boy Thomas had with a woman he was dating when I arrived in Honolulu. The woman passed away and that's why Hope and I flew to Honolulu to be with Thomas. We felt he would need our help. That's how this whole permanent move to Cape St Mary came together. Are you still with me?"

Paradise checked the time. Curtis would expect her to be at the station when he called for her to join him for this pre-arranged evening meeting. One of his men had approached her at her desk mid afternoon to say the Sergeant wanted her in the office right after supper. Seemed less than professional, Paradise had thought, but she did agree to show up and she really should get off the phone and into her car. "I guess I'm just trying to keep you talking so maybe the good-bye won't happen on this call. Maybe when you are here sometime, Paradise, what do you say? Please try to come. Soon, if you can."

"Lenny, I'm sorry, but I need to sign off. I wish you well with WPP and with Bonde for as much time as you have left at 2.0."

As Paradise was about to hang up she heard a very loud and angry voice, a woman's voice. Had someone been listening in on her conversation with Lenny?

40: *You*, get out

Bonde was pissed!

"*This* is how you spend your 'off schedule' time? On the phone with Miss Paradise...love of your life?" Bonde knew she was yelling and was just plain jealous but she wasn't going to let lover-boy get away with stringing her on. "When were you planning to tell me what the hell is going on here?"

In a whisper Len said bye and looked as angry as Bonde felt. "Bye for now, Paradise. I hope to hear from you again. I'm sorry you had to hear that and you probably suspected Bonde had been listening to our conversation. Paradise meet Bonde. Bonde meet Paradise. Not that funny, I guess."

Lenny knew Paradise had already hung up, possibly before Bonde pounced. He tried to savour the goodness in Paradise. He wasn't sure there was much goodness in Bonde but he tried to not compare them...too often. He knew the second his hand was off the telephone receiver he would have to face Bonde. He wasn't wrong.

"Any idea how pathetic you sounded throughout that entire damn call, Len? Oh, excuse me, *Lenny*?"

"Not now, Bonde. Trust me, not now."

"Oh no, you are *not* dismissing me after what I just heard. I wonder if the big boss knows how many long-distance calls you make to your girlfriend in just one shift. I think I need to have a discussion with the Lieutenant Commander in the morning. Want to come along? You might learn something."

"Grow up, Bonde."

"That's rich. You're telling *me* to grow up? You sounded like a love-struck teenager and I thought you might start bawling at the end."

Len was on her in an instant. He stood less than an inch from that intoxicating face but his mind was focused. "How dare you listen in on a private conversation? You go right ahead and talk to Jalen about me, but remember what he said about not going to him with anything related to emotions of any kind. He would give you about ten seconds before booting you out of his office."

"Well look who's all—"

"Shut up. Just shut up. You know what's going on between you and me. It's nothing more than a bit of sex. I have nothing to lose. I'm waiting for my transfer and I'm out of here."

Pointing to the door to his private quarters Len added, "Now, you get out of here. You had no right to come in here when you knew I was on the phone. Go. Just go."

Backing away until she was just outside his open door, Bonde said, "Really, Len, I mean no more to you than that? You see me as nothing more than a quick meet up and a guaranteed orgasm?" Bonde offered a sexy smile with that last comment.

In a much quieter voice Len replied, "My words were unkind, Bonde, and I'm sorry. Really I am. I've got a big issue to be resolved at the moment and it's personal. I will share the ugly details with you when I know more. My hand to God, I will tell you everything. Can we pick this up another time, perhaps before you go to Jalen?"

It was Len's turn to offer a small smile as he reached out and closed the door in her face.

41: Unforgivable lusting

By the time Paradise got to the Sergeant's office door she could see, and hear, that he was in an ugly mood. Paradise was confident she had done nothing wrong so she was pretty sure he wasn't about to be ugly with her.

"What's this meeting about boss?" Paradise asked as she entered with pen and paper in hand, in case he had an assignment for her.

"What's it about? That's rich coming from you, Paradise. You might want to give it a bit more thought."

"I just this second walked into your office and you're upset with me already? I have absolutely no idea what caused this mood of yours, and I certainly don't understand why this is an evening meeting with not one other person in the station." Paradise didn't know what else to say so she took a seat, crossed her legs and stopped talking.

"Let me spell it out for you, then. You, and you alone, are responsible for the breakup of my marriage. The wife knew there was something wrong. She said a woman could always tell when her man was cheating or even *thinking* about cheating. I was spending way more time here at the station and I picked up a new shirt or two, thinking you might like the change, and I even—"

"Stop right there, Curtis. Are you suggesting I'm interested in you on a personal level? My God, you must be joking. Have you been thinking we should cheat on our spouses?"

"So, we're going to play games? We're going to pretend there's no chemistry between us? That you haven't seen, and appreciated, how I look at you? That you haven't nodded in approval when I wear a new shirt? That you didn't know I told the wife about us several weeks ago?" Curtis was running out of things to say and, by the look on her face, Paradise was either a great actress or had actually *not* seen him coming on to her right here at the station. What a mess.

Paradise stood and slowly stepped back toward the door. "Curtis, I did hear via the gossip mill that your wife had moved out and settled somewhere up the line. I also understand she's very happy. Never for a second did I think that had anything to do with me."

"Finally! *Finally* someone admits they know where my wife is staying. Paradise, tell me right this second where the wife is hanging her hat these days, and with who. If you know she is living 'up the line', then you bloody well know where she is living and you can tell me who she is living with." Curtis was around the desk and moving towards Paradise, who was still backing toward the door.

"Stop changing the subject. You said something about telling your wife about us? There is no *us* and I don't know where all this is coming from."

"Liar."

"And calling your wife 'the' wife is derogatory, don't you think? She has a name: use it!"

"Giving me both grammar and marital advice? You are unbelievable! You split us up, then pretend you didn't see it coming. I thought you were better than that and I know *for a fact* you have been coming on to me, no matter what you say."

"Curtis, how can you say this? You're the one who came to me when people at a conference were saying off-colour things about me because of my name. Remember that meeting? You suggested we change my name, for working purposes only. Paradise would become P d, do you remember it now? You had my back, so what changed?"

Paradise was almost in tears but she wouldn't let that happen, not here. "You even bought me a box of business cards with the name change. I do remember thinking what a kind gesture that was, but at no time have I ever been attracted to you."

Curtis drew himself up. "Many people have told me how attractive I am."

"Oh, you're an attractive man, but you know what I'm trying to say. And your wife is absolutely beautiful inside and out. She always showed great respect for everyone working in the office when she came to see you. I guess she hasn't dropped in for some time, now that I think about it."

"Look at you backing away from me, Paradise. You are just too sweet. You're not frightened of the big bad boss now, are you?"

"No."

"Liar."

Then they heard a car pull into the pebble parking lot behind the station. Curtis paused in mid-step, listening intently. Paradise calculated the distance to the door.

Then they heard the outer door open and Thomas' voice. "Time check, Paradise. That's it, my love. Time to call it a night."

Before Curtis could react, Paradise stepped out into the hall and waved. "Thomas, down here. I was just about to share our news with Curtis. Come on in with me so we can share together."

By the time Thomas entered the office, with a raised eyebrow from him and a small shrug in response from Paradise, Curtis had composed himself a bit and was back by his desk. "Hey the more the merrier, Thomas, come on in. We were just about to call it a day so how about a night-cap?"

"Sounds great," Thomas said.

"Not a chance, gentlemen," Paradise mock-scolded. "This won't take a minute."

With a question on his face that only Paradise could see, Thomas sat down but said nothing.

Looking directly at her boss, Paradise said, "This time I'll address you as Sergeant Curtis, to formalize what I am about to say."

"Should I put on my hat and jacket?" Curtis asked.

"No, sir."

There was an eddy of silence. Then Paradise drew breath. "I am offering my resignation from the Cape St Mary police force, effective two weeks from today, per my contract with you. Given the content of our discussion earlier this evening, and in particular your accusations and you luring me here when there would be no one else in the building, my preference is to leave immediately. If that happens, I will expect to receive full pay for the next two weeks. Finally, I want on the record that I have found you to be totally unprofessional during this meeting, with your suggestions of there ever being an 'us' as a couple. Your thought process frightens me. You are in charge of the Cape police force and, at this moment, I don't think you are capable of fulfilling your duties."

Curtis turned to Thomas and said, "Did you know your little wife here has been coming on to me at the office? She even came between my wife and me. Veronica and I are separated at the moment, and that's all on Miss perfect here. Isn't that right, Paradise?"

Thomas got to his feet. "Our daughter would say, 'Oh. My. God.' Paradise, gather up all your files, and I do mean *all* of your files, and we're out of here. I'll let you get started while I have a few words with the Sergeant if you don't mind."

"Should I stay?" Paradise said.

"No," and, "no" from both men and Paradise was in motion, heading to her office.

En route she picked up a few sturdy case-file boxes to hold her personal belongings. She was thankful she had not let her files accumulate at the station. It was uncomfortable packing while resisting the urge to go back and see what was happening.

"Thomas," Curtis said, "I'm a bit stunned. Did Paradise leave home today with thoughts of resigning? I have worked hard to open doors for your woman and this is how she treats me? And she definitely has been flirting with me."

Thomas slowly put his hands in his pockets, where they could not reach Curtis's neck. "You may not know that our private business has been building. Over the past few months our caseload has more than doubled"

"Then why didn't she say so?"

"I think she did, if you had been listening."

"Don't go putting anything on me!"

"What I will be putting on you is a report to your superiors." Thomas took a step forward, causing the sergeant to move back.

"There are so many things Paradise could charge you with. Perhaps you could direct your energy to your career and to the mess you have made of your personal life. Your unforgivable lusting after Paradise stops right here right now."

"But I didn't—"

"Save it for your disciplinary hearing, pal."

Thomas left the office with the studied, slow gait of a man who is on the verge of losing it. He walked down the hall without looking back and made his way to where Paradise was forcing a lid on a box.

"Who's watching the children, Thomas?"

"Hope was still awake so I asked her to give me 20 minutes or so to pick you up."

Thomas picked some boxes. "Grab that last one, sweetheart, and we're gone."

With a drink in hand, Curtis tried to fill his office door as Paradise and Thomas walked past. They didn't even glance his way.

He filled his glass for the second or third time. He had lost count.

42: Favourite soup

"Could we take the boat out one day soon, Pops? I know you're not keen to do that but maybe we could use the opportunity to do something nice for someone. We could invite Eugenie and make it a surprise for her. What do you think?"

Hope was excited about the possibility. She wouldn't pressure Pops, though, because she didn't want it to be an emotionally-charged day. Hope was assuming Eugenie had not been serious about being sick while out on the beautiful ocean. "Eugenie is always asking us what we do when we head down to your boat, so don't you think she would feel proud if we made it all about her for once? Being a nun. I guess she wasn't pampered too much. I find Eugenie's stories about her life 'on the inside' fascinating. Pops. Do you know she didn't even own a mirror? Not even a tiny little one."

Hope figured she had overstated her idea, so she sat on her hands and said no more. After a few seconds, she added, "Over to you, Pops." Okay, *now* she would say no more.

"I'm all for it, Hope, and it's a great idea. Can we add a fourth person?"

"Of course. Who did you have in mind, Pops?"

"Actually, I was thinking of your mom. I've never taken her out on my boat. When we were first getting to know each other and long before I knew the details I would later learn, like about your birth for example, we would meet down on the wharf near my boat and she would ask questions about her mother and father. I would try so hard to make it all fit together properly. I sometimes couldn't even show up for our meeting because I knew it was one of the days I had to talk about my Cole and I knew I couldn't get through that without crying. I even practised what I might want to say next time I saw her, but that didn't help much. I felt some bad for not showing up on those days, though."

Hope couldn't believe what she was hearing. "*Crying*? You were afraid you might end up crying?"

"Hope, go careful on this old man. I didn't learn a man could cry and not be embarrassed until your mother taught me all about feelings."

"Hey, let's do it today, Pops. What do you say?"

"Oh, I don't know, Hope, I might like to clean her up a bit. I just did a bit of painting on her the other day and I want to go down and check it out."

"Pops, I know you. Every day that we put it off you will find more and more work you want to do on her."

"No, she's pretty much ready now, just this one thing for me to check out, that's all."

Hope noticed that Pops was in a very good mood at the moment and that gave her an idea. She figured it would be an easy sell. "Pops, why don't we do this: You go on down to your 'girl' and I'll see if I can coax Eugenie to come and then I'll ask mom."

"It's a date, young lady, I'll pick up coffee and a bit of grub from Café Central and I'll be waiting for you three ladies down on the dock."

Hope was long gone before Pops had finished what he was saying. She did that all the time and it always made him smile.

She's some girl, our young Hope. Every time Pops made a plan to do something with Hope, she was off and running to ask Paradise if it was okay, or to explain where she was going with him.

More than an hour passed, with Pops wondering why the ladies hadn't arrived, when suddenly he saw two but not three hustling along the wharf. Hope began talking as soon as she felt he could hear her so she was actually shouting not talking.

Pops was used to it but sometimes he didn't hear so good. He made a note to talk with Hope about how she could help him learn to live with his hearing loss.

"Pops I can't find mom. She was meeting someone for lunch today but I forget who she told me it was."

Hope and Eugenie had caught up with Pops and with some difficulty Eugenie sat on the stump beside him. "Hey, Eugenie, good genes right there." Hope was impressed by how easily Eugenie sat down, and wanted to compliment her.

Turning to Pops, she added, "You too, Pops. Now let's talk about what we're going to do today."

"Sit down for a second, Hope. Everything is going to be just fine. I have observed, young lady, that sometimes when your mom is telling you something, you are multitasking and I'm not sure you listen."

"Well I'm not sure you should be calling me out on whether or not I always listen to my mother when we're meant to have lunch on this beautiful boat once we get out there on the big old ocean. You're right, though. I should listen better and I will, I promise."

Hope was still standing, but Pops and Eugenie didn't seem too eager to get up and actually board the boat. Hope was a bit surprised that Pops wasn't already on board. She should have seen this coming.

"What an idiot I am, Pops. I think I know why you're still sitting on your favourite stoop. I'll just mosey on over here to my very own stoop and sit."

Hope was near tears so Pops knew he had to speak up. She had him all figured out. "Eugenie and Hope, I know this was my idea and I came on down here and I tried. Honest to your God, Eugenie, I really thought I could take us all out for a sea-spin and we could throw our anchor at some point and have our lunch."

"What are you telling us, my love?" Eugenie was concerned. Pops looked like he was in pain. "Are you feeling sick and don't want us to know, or is it possibly related to your beloved Cole? Is he on your mind?"

"Give the lady a prize. She guessed correctly."

"That's a bit insensitive, don't you think, Hope?" Pops was cross with her for that quick-witted comment...*time and place and this isn't the time*, he thought.

"I want to say I'm sorry to both of you." Hope was trying to get this party back on track but it didn't seem to be working. "Pops, I knew you were thinking about Cole. And, Eugenie, I shouldn't have made light of your comment. But can we please get going even if we go aboard and just eat our snacks by the dock?"

Eugenie shook her head. "Hope, I wasn't kidding when I shared with you that I get very seasick. I have tried just sitting in it with Pops but I have to throw up with the first wave that comes near. Pops, you don't know this, but I have even come down to the boat when you are busy somewhere else and tried to sit on board and keep my lunch down...not possible."

She spread her hands in a hopeless gesture. "So my plan today was to come down here and see the three of you off, so why don't we forget about boarding and have snacks while we sit on these comfortable stoops. Although, Hope, you are too far away from us sitting over there."

"Easy to fix," Hope said as she moved to their side and sat on the wharf between them. She crossed her legs and asked, "So what are we snacking on and where is it?"

43: Parlour and Rapure

On impulse Elise had invited Paradise to her home for lunch. They had a lot of fun talking about their pending luncheon date. "Paradise, would you fancy coming to lunch in the parlour with me? I'm just being silly when I say 'in the parlour' because my parlour is my bedroom, kitchen, and my entire living space. The kids insisted on me living in the addition to their house for as long as I was independent and so far so good."

"I would be delighted!"

And today was the day. Elise rushed to the door to invite her young friend in. Paradise was the daughter of her very best friend, Madeline, who had died giving birth to Paradise.

The minute Paradise stepped inside she could smell the aroma coming from Elise's oven in the corner, beside what she assumed was a sofa that clearly doubled as a bed. The place was so clean Paradise was sure they could eat off the floor if necessary.

"Come and sit at the table, Paradise. Lunch is ready and I have a good reason for seating and serving you here at the table right away. As you can see, the only other place to sit is over there on the sofa. I thought we could sit there and have a coffee later."

"Elise, I am so touched to be inside your little home, because the gossip cavalry tells me this is not something you do all the time. Have a friend in for lunch, I mean."

Paradise sat in a pretty chair with a bright red and yellow cushion for comfort. Elise would have the other chair, sporting a red and blue cushion. Paradise could see that Elise was not paying particular attention to her as she served up lunch, so she sat quietly.

"Paradise, over the years, you have expressed an interest in learning how to make Rapure. You call it Rappie pie in English, I believe. I remember you asking me about Rapure when we first met."

"Oh, I don't know about that. I said I would love to *eat* Rapure made the way my mother would have made it."

"I finally do believe you when you say you do not cook or bake. Both Hope and Thomas have confirmed this. All in good humour, I mean."

Elise made her way over to Paradise with a beautiful, hand-painted bowl filled to the brim. You could warm your hands when you put them around the bowl.

Paradise inhaled and said, "I might be convinced to learn how to make this, but not today. Not today." Paradise wiped an early tear from her face. "We're going to talk about my mom like we always do, correct?"

"Of course we are, dear, I really was kidding you about learning to make this for your family. But...can I just tell you a little bit about Rapure while we dig in? Oh, pardon me, I made bread but it's still in the warming oven. I'll just grab it." Elise scurried to the stove and back again.

"I'm so impressed with how easily you move around, Elise," Paradise added with love in her voice.

"In my home, yes, but when I'm outside and walkways are not as flat and smooth as my floor is, it's another story. My age has crept up on me. No complaints, though. I'm doing good."

"Forgive me if I'm being too personal, but I see a cane propped up against your bed. I don't think I have seen you using a cane."

"Paradise, what you're really saying is that you hear me say I'm doing good yet you see a cane. Not to worry my young friend, I saw it at Frenchys for a dollar so I thought I might decorate with it until I am forced to use it as it's intended. To help me get around, I mean. Nothing more than that, I promise."

"If you say so. Do you want to begin with another favourite story about my mother?" Paradise was always anxious to begin their conversation so she could continue to learn as much as possible about her mom.

Elise laughed. "In a minute, Paradise. I am going to spend a minute or two talking about Rapure, even if it kills me!" Paradise laughed. "This is delicious so I promise to sit quietly and eat my dinner while you tell me how you made it. How does that sound?"

"Finally!" Elise tried to make it a short story because she was hungry too. "Rapure is a well-loved Acadian dish. Every Acadian knows all about Rapure and, I don't know this for sure, but I bet most Acadians know how to make it."

Paradise, laughing again, said, "That's not a slag at us English folk, is it?"

"Of course not. You know that, Paradise. So, as I was saying... Rapure is a delicious mix of potatoes and chicken. I suspect it's a local dish and unique to our region. In the conventional sense this is not a pie because there is no pastry crust involved..." It was not lost on Elise that Paradise appeared to be thinking of something else. Probably her mother, so she tried to bring her mom into her story.

"Sorry Elise, I wandered off there for a second."

"I know you did, dear, but let me continue, please. My mother taught me how to make Rapure and then I taught Madeline. I always say mom taught me how to do this, but as you know from one of our previous discussions your mother and mine died when we were very young. I realize my 'presentation' of all-things-Rapure sounds like nothing more than absolute drivel but your mother would, at the very least, expect me to teach you how to make this dish. If that was lost on you, so be it."

With her hands outstretched Elsie wrapped it up. "My teaching days are now over, what would you like the revised subject matter to be, Paradise? Over to you."

44: No mother and no money

"I do remember," Paradise said, "you explaining how mom and you were very poor and whenever you heard the other girls in class talk about asking their mom for more money, you and my mom would put your heads together and quote your own personal motto. I don't remember the motto though."

"No mother. No money," Elise replied, bursting into tears.

"I'm so sorry, Elise, let's sit quietly for a minute and enjoy this wonderful Rapure and, goodness, this homemade bread is heavenly."

"Thank you, dear. I still miss your mother after all these years. When I see your face, Paradise, and hear your voice, it's as if it's Madeline right here beside me. Just like we were then...best friends forever."

Starting to cry again, Elise poked fun at herself. "I should have taken your advice to sit quietly...since it's clear I didn't understand the 'quietly' part."

"Let me tell you what I've decided as I sit here enjoying this wonderful dinner with you" Paradise said. "I *do not* need to learn how to bake bread and now that I see what a wonderful cook you are I have no interest in learning any of it. A girl can't do everything, you know. I don't-do kitchen and I say that proudly."

They were both laughing. "How would you like to earn a bit of money, Elsie? I'm serious when I say this. I could order home-cooked meals from you and then I could serve them in my home. Please say yes. Please tell me you love to cook and bake as well."

Paradise knew she sounded downright giddy and she was okay with that. The possibilities were endless!

"Paradise, would you like more Rapure before we continue?"

"My land, no, I couldn't eat another thing at the moment. Thank you for this beautiful meal."

"It's not over yet. Let me put some water on the stove to boil. We need a good cup of coffee to go with the cherry crumble I have made for us. It's one of my most asked-for dishes when I meet up with anyone in my family for a meal and I ask what I can bring to contribute. Did that sound like bragging?"

"If it did, you have reason to brag, Elise. I would shout it from the rooftops if I could make anything but a reservation. That's what I make when it's my turn to treat someone to a meal."

"Time to get serious," Elise said. "Remind me where you want me to start or what you might like me to repeat about your mom and me."

"Surprise me. I'm already in tears and yet I keep asking you to tell me more. If I really want to cry I guess you could talk about the day I was born and mom died. Those visuals are in my head, but hearing about that day makes me love my mother a little bit more each time I think about the details of it all."

Elise could see that Paradise wanted to say something else, so she busied herself with her cherry crumble and her now-empty coffee cup. "Are you sure, Paradise?"

Paradise smiled. "You know me so well, and that in itself is incredible. You look at me and hear my mom and I listen to you describe in such detail the many times you and my mom were together. I close my eyes and have the visual to go with your story."

Paradise paused to sip her coffee...Elise made excellent coffee. "If I recap, it's sad, but it's the story of how two young girls became friends and that friendship grew and flourished until the day mom died. You were poor but happy. You both lost your mother at a very young age. Cole began to invade the space you shared with mom, yet your friendship was so strong you never felt jealous or threatened. When my mother became pregnant with me, she and Cole moved in with Pops and the men fished together. They married and made plans to finish their education, raise a family and possibly travel if Cole ended up with a career that paid well. How am I doing so far?"

Paradise wondered if she had said something that upset Elise, because she had a frown on her face. And, sure enough…

"To be honest with you, I didn't like it when you talked about me not being jealous or threatened when Cole and your mom fell in love. If it's true that you don't think I was jealous or felt threatened, why do you even say it? I didn't like that one little bit." Elise was looking down at the floor and avoiding any eye contact with Paradise."You're absolutely right, Elise. I misspoke and I'm sorry. I hope you will accept my apology."

Elsie reached out and gave Paradise a big hug. "Apology accepted. Would this count as our first fight?"

"My fault, so I'll make sure we never have a second fight."

Elise sat smiling and Paradise realized she had gone back in time just for a second and saw her friend Madeline smiling back at her.

"Elise, I am just noticing the time, and I need to get home to check on Thomas and Lee. I said I would be back long before now. I also need to check and see what my very busy daughter has gotten up to. She has no school today so she and Pops were going to make plans. Is it okay with you if we pick this up next time?"

"I look forward to that. And if you enjoyed spending time here I would love to continue to host our lunches. What is it you called our meetings? *Lunch 'n Learn* or something like that?"

"The lunch was fantastic and I would love to return to your lovely little home soon. Very soon! I'm leaving you with a sink full of dishes, though, so maybe I won't run off quite so quickly."

"Oh, yes you will, young lady. Dirty dishes give me something to do, so off you go right this minute."

Friends forever, Elise thought as she watched through the kitchen window as Paradise made her way home. She knew she could never fill Madeline's shoes, but every minute spent with Paradise was rewarding in a way Elise could hardly believe. She knew she would meet up with Madeline again one day. She would have so much to tell her best friend.

They were kids when Madeline died, yet Elise had never met anyone who could replace her forever-best friend.

45: What fright looks like

Russ and Carol were playing matchmaker and they weren't at all sure things would go as they hoped.

"Who do we talk to first?" Russ said. "I saw both Denis and Waine walking on the beach this morning. I may just be hoping that Waine is feeling better, but for certain he walked much farther this morning than any other morning."

Russ had gotten to know the brothers during the evening, when his chores were done for the day. He knew Denis and Waine would be sitting outside until at least sunset and they always invited him to join them for a beer. Russ would *never* refuse a beer.

"We haven't seen the doctor's car for a few days, so maybe Waine is on-the-mend and will soon be ready to meet his nephew. I think it speaks volumes about the support Denis gives Waine. Denis told me that they would meet their nephew when his brother was ready. I think they are good men. I want to do something nice for them. Is that so bad? What could go wrong?" Carol felt she had to speak up even though she knew Russ's heart was in the right place. "Calm down, cowboy," she drawled, knowing the expression would make him laugh. Worked every time. "What makes you think you have the right to show up at their cottage with their nephew? I think they're nervous about it and don't want to screw up. It's *their* surprise. And it's *their* plan, Russ. This is their personal, and at the moment sad, trip. Talk to them about it, but please don't do anything unless they ask you too."

Carol knew Russ was waiting for her to leave him alone. She spoke what was in her heart and then, as she did every evening, she left for her daily run along Mavillette beach.

Russ decided he would sleep on his idea. But tomorrow would

be the day he did something to help Denis and Waine, and he wanted that to include their nephew.

Dreams and good intentions are sometimes shattered by reality, and that's what Russ woke up to the following morning. Not even daylight yet and the doctor's car was parked in front of Waine and Denis's cabin. He might be wrong, didn't have his glasses on, but Russ thought the car had been parked on the tiny patch of grass directly in front of the cabin where Denis sat once Waine was tucked into bed. Not wanting to wake him up, Denis pretty much always moved his lawn chair from their deck to the grass below.

"Call me nosy, but, by God, I'm going over there with three hot cups of coffee...four including mine. There could be something I can do to help."

Carol might not have heard exactly what Russ had said but when she pulled the curtain back in their upstairs bedroom she saw him gingerly walk up the steps to the cabin door, balancing coffees and hot muffins for everyone.

Denis met Russ at the screen door and said, "Give me a second. I'll come out, but first give me two of those coffees and I'll pass them on to Doctor Legault and my brother."

The two coffees had cooled somewhat when Denis reappeared on the deck. He slumped into a chair as if his strings had been cut.

Russ jumped in first because he felt he should. "Denis, you don't have to tell me anything about what's going on. I just wanted to help, and if all you need is the coffee and these muffins just say so and I'll head back to the office."

"Russ, I wish to God there was something you or I could do for my brother. We went to bed last night after reviewing our plans for today. Plans that included meeting our nephew for the first time. Waine was doing so well and we had the 'all clear' from his doctor that we could meet family. When we said goodnight we were happy. So happy."

Denis looked at his coffee as if wondering how it had appeared in his hand. He set it down on the deck rail. "I got up around three to use the washroom and I found my poor sod of a brother in a pool of his own blood on the bathroom floor. I thought he was dead. There was so much blood. He had slit both wrists, Russ. Who does that after going to bed happy?"

Denis began to weep and stood up, or tried to.

"Don't go, Denis. Please. I've seen mental health issues and I know what fright looks like when someone you love is spiralling out of control. We can talk about things another time."

"...okay."

Russ released the breath he had been holding. "Okay, then. For today, uh, do you all need more coffee?"

Denis nodded. "We sure do. Thanks a million. And, can you hurry, please?"

Russ saw a tiny smile and knew Denis was sad but he was definitely okay. He prayed Waine would be okay too.

Russ ran directly across his well-kept lawn. He didn't want to waste a second. He was thankful no guests had arrived for their complimentary breakfast as he rushed through the door and went looking for Carol.

"I need you to handle everything here, honey. Denis asked if I could bring more coffee and stay for awhile."

It was just a harmless little lie. Russ knew that Carol knew. She would let him get away with it...for now.

46: Fat like you

"Let's make sure you're comfortable, Waine." Denis fussed around his brother while Russ and Doctor Legault talked.

"Can't tell you a damn thing, Russ. Not my place, so please don't put me on the spot."

Doctor Legault was a bit surprised by all the questions Russ was asking. He didn't mind talking with the man, and clearly both Denis and Waine were comfortable around Russ, but it was their story to share. "I know your heart is in the right place. As Denis has told you, a man almost died in this cabin a few hours ago. That same man is now begging me not to have him transferred to our mental health facility in Halifax. That all adds up to me staying right here for now. I won't be part of the convoy heading over to Cape St Mary Road, but I won't be calling for an ambulance either. The boys have asked me to stay until the big 'Lee reveal'. That now includes you, too."

"Carol didn't want me to come over, and I'll be getting a hot tongue and cold shoulder from her if this gets out. I'm some sorry, Doctor, and I promise to be as quiet as a mouse when we return with little Lee."

Doctor Legault gave Russ a pat on the shoulder. "Let's not go overboard, son. I'm not a betting man, but I'm almost willing to bet you have never in your life been quiet as a mouse."

Russ was quick to whisper, "Don't do 'overboard' jokes around Pops, whatever you do—"

Doctor Legault said quickly, "The expression was out of my mouth before I remembered the story about Cole. I'll be beating myself up over that one for a long time."

He gave himself a little shake, as if shedding a coat. "If we're through here, I'm off to check on Waine."

~

Some time passed before Russ heard the screen door open and stopped his pacing. Denis came out. Alone.

"Has there been a change in plans? Where's Waine?"

"Russ, I need you to let me be in charge here. You asking a million questions has me rattled and I don't want the boy to see me this way. For God's sake, my hands are shaking. Now let's get going before I chicken out."

"Is it just you and I going to 548?" This had been the first suggestion Russ had thrown out but...oh no...it was a bad idea at the time, yet here they were doing exactly what he said in the first place.

"Looks like."

Russ offered Denis a small smile and a nod, then left to bring his car around. He had offered to drive in case Lee came back with them. That way Denis could focus on the boy.

548 Cape St Mary Road was not that far, so they were turning into the driveway in less than five minutes.

Denis wasn't expecting this. "Is this it? My goodness, Russ, I thought getting here would take a bit longer and I would have time to collect my thoughts."

"I could drive around a bit."

"No, no. I'm fine."

They sat in silence for a bit. Then Russ said quietly, "I never heard a guy as big as you say 'my goodness' before."

"Well...Waine and I swore if we could meet our nephew we would never swear again."

"Everything will be just fine, Denis. Trust me."

As they got out of the car, Russ noticed four people sitting on the veranda as if watching for them. He suspected Carol had called Paradise. That just might have been the best idea anyone had all morning.

Paradise was the first to step up and approach them. "Hello,

Russ. What brings you to our doorstep and who's your friend?"

Paradise knew perfectly well who the 'friend', was but she needed time to settle her nerves. Thomas, Paradise and Hope had tried so hard to find Wikolia's family before moving to Cape St Mary, and now it would appear Wikolia's family had found them.

"Paradise, rather than just telling *you* a great story, could we talk with all four of you?" Russ decided there was safety in numbers. "You won't be disappointed I promise. This man and his brother have come a very long way to meet all of you."

"Denis," Paradise raised her voice slightly so the others, especially Lee, could hear. "I'm not sure if you are Denis or Waine, sir, but I'm Paradise and I'm thrilled to meet you. We all are."

"I'm Denis. Thank you for the kind words. Can I meet the rest of the family?"

It was Lee who brought the family together, as only a young child can do. "Sir, you kinda' look like me. I'm not fat like you but our skin is kind of the same colour. Do I look like you?"

Lee was off the porch steps and bouncing up and down as he took Paradise's hand. "Mommy, do you think I look a little bit like this old man? Oh frig, I just remember I shouldn't have called him fat, right Mommy?"

"Hello, young man. My name is Denis and did I hear you call me fat?"

Denis was joking with his nephew, but he was also giving himself time. He needed his words to catch up with his heart.

47: Tattletale presentation

Jalen waited before speaking. He wasn't sure Bonde was finished. For her own good, she better be. She certainly could run-off at the mouth.

Bonde had already caught the eye of a number of men on his payroll with Len being at the top of the list if the rumours were true. Jalen was tempted to ask Bonde if she always dressed the way she was dressed today, but he wasn't sure he wanted to hear her answer.

Ten seconds after she entered his office she had claimed she was 'so hot' that she had to remove her jacket. She did that during a best-delivered-out-of-the-office striptease performance revealing a strapless dress with nothing underneath it. *Nothing.* Certainly she was not wearing a bra. Jalen suspected, given the size of her breasts, it must hurt to just let them hang loose that way. Then, he decided the answer to *that* question was well above his pay grade so he tried to get his mind back on the job before him.

"You're finished I assume?"

Following her cheeky nod, Jalen continued. "So what you're telling me is that you caught 'Lenny', in his own private corner of the warehouse, talking on the phone with Paradise, who happens to be a good friend of his. Is that about it?" Jalen had had just about all he could take from this employee. "Do I detect a hint of jealousy in your voice and perhaps in your decision to put on a performance just now?"

"So you did notice? I wondered. You could have fooled me. I normally get a reaction but in your case, I got nothin'. Nada."

Bonde was squirming a bit, and perhaps she was telling tales out of school but Jalen deserved to know what Lenny was doing behind his back. Oh sure, he was on his own time. With permission to call anywhere he wanted. Blah. Blah Blah. How was Bonde to know this was Lenny's first long distance call? She didn't believe that nugget of information, but she knew when she was beaten, so she would fight that fight another day.

This isn't over, she thought, but she kept herself in check and didn't say it out loud. She hadn't realized just how tight Jalen and Lenny seemed to be.

Jalen's immediate reaction to Bonde's 'employee information,' which was how she prefaced her tattletale presentation, had been to fire her on the spot. He pondered that plan as he listened to Bonde go on and on. What she didn't realize was that Jalen continued to have Lenny's back. That would never change, and he was keen to share this little nugget with Lenny.

It seemed that Lenny had a 'thing' for his workmates. Perhaps Jalen would fire Bonde and replace her with a man...

Finding a way to get Bonde the hell out of his office was not a simple task. She unsettled Jalen in a way he wasn't used to and he certainly couldn't act on. Since his wife's death a number of years ago he had dated; but never, absolutely never, would Jalen date a 5.0 or 2.0 employee.

She was a sexy woman, she knew it, and she wasn't beneath using her sex appeal to unsettle a man.

But Bonde sealed her own fate when she asked, "Do you want me to go and get Lenny? He doesn't know I'm in your office, but I did warn him that I would be talking to you. He told me to 'go right ahead', but I could tell he was hoping I was all talk and no action. He was sure that nothing would come of me talking with you. So should I go and get him for you?"

"Great idea, Bonde. Send him in. You don't need to join us. Lenny and I are due to have a bit of a man-to-man talk."

"Whatever are you asking, Lieutenant Commander? *Man-to-man* is a foreign concept to me."

Jalen had said all he planned to say to Bonde. He opened a file on his desk, and Bonde, thankfully, took that as her cue to leave.

Deciding a 'heads-up' was only fair Jalen picked up the phone and placed an internal call. When the call was answered, Jalen said only, "Bonde is on her way to your quarters. Once she gets there and says her piece, I want you in my office. Do *not* bring that woman with you."

48: PIU—the Cape Crew

Thomas knew their 'shingle; was a bit cheeky. "You're okay with this, right, honey? It's intended to make the boys smile. We can take it down after they arrive, so no harm done."

He looked into Paradise's eyes and saw she got the joke. The office in Ontario boasted a fairly large sign that read *PIU – Private Investigators Unlimited*. As their friends drove into their driveway, Thomas knew Clint and Jim would easily relate to their shingle, *PIU...the Cape Crew*.

"It's perfect," Paradise replied.

They had been thinking of hanging up their sign ever since they moved back to the Cape. Paradise no longer worked with Curtis at the Cape police force so the time was right. In fact, rumour in the village was that Curtis might be relieved of his duties. This saddened Paradise. She felt Curtis needed some sensitivity training and a few related courses, but she would feel badly if he was fired as a result of her single complaint.

Thanks to Doctor Sydney Scott, Paradise had been able to take several courses related to forensics and investigative work that might one day open the doors for her to become a for-real detective. "Watch me," she said to Thomas whenever he teased her about her 'lofty' goals.

"Woman, you will succeed no matter what route you take. Just save enough time for the kids and me when you have that big job."

"Never mind my goals, Thomas. Is our shingle straight on the post? We don't want it to be off-centre and blowing in the wind when the boys arrive."

The "boys" from the Ontario office were coming to the Cape during a well-deserved vacation. They had decided to fly from Toronto to Halifax rather than drive. They would then rent a fancy car and explore Nova Scotia en route to their partners in Cape St Mary. No timetable, no map, no worry. They would get there whenever...

Thomas was happy to be reconnecting with his partner, Clint, who had quit the training program with the Royal Canadian Mounted Police at the same time Thomas left. Neither liked the structure they would have had to live by if they stuck with the RCMP. They quickly formed a two-man business called PIU and worked together until Thomas's life took him to Hawaii. It would be nice to reunite and also meet Clint's business and life partner, Jim Taylor.

"Now there's a story," Thomas said, not realizing he had spoken loud enough for Paradise to hear.

"What is our position considering their personal lifestyle anyway, Thomas? It's illegal, I know, but it's their business not ours, correct?"

"Correct, my love. But it's not our position I'm concerned about. The world isn't ready to acknowledge and accept same-sex marriage, and I don't know if it ever will be. Clint and Jim don't flaunt their love for each other, but that's not saying someone won't, one day, call them on it. I know they won't lie when confronted, and in the wrong situation they would not be safe. They would not be safe at all, and that worries me."

"Let's talk about this on their first day with us. We will support them any way we can, but we need to know up front what we can do to make life easy for them here in the Cape, and when they travel back to Ontario." Paradise went on to add, "And anywhere else they may go for as long as it takes for the world to be more accepting."

"I wish everyone had a heart as big as yours, Paradise." With that, the shingle was nailed to the house and Thomas concluded with, "It's in place and it's straight—no pun intended."

49: He's bawling, Dad

Before kneeling down to talk directly with the child, Denis whispered to Paradise and Thomas, "I heard him call you mommy. Does this mean I shouldn't speak of my sister...his mother?"

"We speak of Wikolia in heaven often," Thomas murmured, "so maybe you could refer to her that way. Nothing you say will be wrong. Just be natural."

"Easy for you to say," Denis offered with a smile.

He took a knee to be at eye level with Lee, then, seeing that he was still much taller than the child, he sat on the ground in front of him. He knew that getting up would not be pretty, but he was too excited as he looked at Lee to worry about embarrassing himself later.

"Lee, thank you for speaking to me this morning. I have wanted to meet you since the day I learned of your birth."

Not realizing he was interrupting this big man, Lee just had to say, "I got borned four years ago. I'm not free anymore, I'm four." He held up four fingers to prove his point.

Not trying to hide the tears in his eyes, Denis went on, "And I see you're a very happy boy. You have a beautiful smile, Lee. I might add, I did look more like you when I was a little boy around the same age. You definitely got those dark eyes from my sister, Wikolia. That I am sure of."

"Hey, do you mean my mommy in heaven? Do you know her? She has a hard name to say, like the one you just said but I call her mommy and that's not a hard word at all because I have two mommies. One in heaven and, look, one right here." Of course Lee was pointing at Paradise.

"You are such a big boy Lee, and you are so smart." Denis was still trying to compose himself.

Seeing the tears, Lee moved over tentatively and sat on the stranger's lap while looking over, first at his mommy and then at Thomas. "He's bawling, Dad, so is it okay if I sit here until he stops?"

Not sure if it would be appropriate to hug the child, Denis did so anyway while saying loud enough for Lee's family to hear, "You're right, Lee. *I am bawling.* And I'll likely keep bawling for days, but I'm trying hard to quit. I'll tell you what would cheer me up. Why don't you tell me a joke? Do you know any jokes?"

"Sure. Knock Knock."

"Who's there?"

Lee looked at his sister. Clearly he had nothing more to say.

"Hi Denis, I'm Lee's sister, Hope. I'm so happy to meet you, sir. We're still working on the next part of our joke."

Turning to Lee, Hope went on, "We can't share this joke until we remember the reply. Look at me, Lee. We talked about needing to learn more about 'the punch line' before you tell the joke, do you remember?"

"No. Well, maybe I do remember what you said but he laughed anyway, so 'Knock Knock' must be funny, right?"

Lee then gave Denis a shoulder shrug and a blank look as if to say, "Over to you, Buddy. I've got nothin'."

Denis had control of his emotions at this point so he was able to take the lead from Lee, even if he was a hard act to follow. "Lee, my brother, Waine, and I came all the way from Hawaii to meet you. Do you know where Hawaii is, son?"

"I got borned in Hawaii but I'm not your son." Lee looked more confused than frightened,' so Denis tried again.

"Sorry, s—" He caught himself at the last second. "Sorry, Lee. Sometimes I get my words wrong."

"Me too, right, Hope?"

Sitting down beside her brother and this big guy, Hope said, "Lee, you are very good with your words, but you know we are working on not interrupting someone else when they are talking, correct?"

Lee didn't speak but did nod his head.

"Oh, great, now you're quiet."

Hope reached over, picked Lee up and sat him on her lap facing Denis. This way she could, she hoped, help him control his interruptions. She gave Denis a nod.

"I'll try to make this real quick—"

"Hey Denis, I can run real quick watch." Lee was out of Hope's arms before she could tighten her grip on him.

Paradise came to the rescue. "If you're up to it, how about a short walk on the beach? Lee is at his best when he's in motion and he might even answer your questions, too. In the interim I'm sure Thomas and I can fill in a few of the blanks concerning your sister. We are so sorry for your loss, by the way. Hope was very close to Wikolia and I know she would welcome your presence here with us for as long as you can stay."

"Who needs to go to the bathroom?" Thomas motioned for Hope to go with her brother.

"Dad, can I bring all of my toys?"

"No toys, Lee. Go to the bathroom and take your sister with you. Come right back, okay, kids?"

"A quick chat before they return," Paradise said. "Is your brother joining us, and what about you, Russ? I know walking the beach isn't your favourite thing. You're welcome to stay here if you like."

Turning to Thomas, Russ said, "If you could drive Denis back to the cottage when he's ready to go, I really should head back to the office to help Carol. We have a number of cabins and motel rooms to clean before our next bookings arrive."

Thomas said he would gladly be the designated driver.

Denis quickly added, "Russ, check on Waine, will you, please? And tell Doctor Legault what is going on over here. We won't be long."

With that Denis suggested he should get back to his brother soon, but he would appreciate a short beach walk for now.

It was not lost on Paradise or Thomas that Denis didn't look like he did much walking. Weight training, maybe, or boxing, but they weren't sure. That might be a good starting point once they made it down to the beach and tried to open the discussion as they followed along behind Lee. He would be running away and coming back and running away and coming back so how fast anyone else walked didn't matter to Lee. He had one speed only...fast.

Hope and Lee returned in beachwear, with towels and obviously raring to go. "We both washed our hands," Lee said, "so you don't need to ask us that, Mom. If you don't have to pee, sir, we can get going now."

Paradise offered an olive branch. "Lee, Denis isn't 'sir'. He's your uncle, my love, so you can call him 'Uncle Denis'. And, Hope, I don't think Denis will mind if you call him Uncle as well. I hope I'm not speaking out of turn," Paradise said as she realized Denis was crying again.

"Denis, did you already know you're my uncle? *Why* are you my uncle? I don't get it." Lee seemed confused but not upset. "Do you get it, sir?"

Denis took charge. "Because, your mother, who now lives in heaven, is my sister. That's what makes me your uncle."

Turning to Paradise, Denis quickly added, "I'm all out of tears, so please get me to the beach. *Please!*"

Over the next hour, with Hope keeping an eye on Lee, Denis learned more from Paradise and Thomas. He didn't ask why Thomas broke up with Wikolia. He put it all together when Paradise shared that she was Hope's mother. Denis hadn't known that. he and Waine had so much to learn.

50: Cabin #3

Russ climbed the steps two at a time, but stopped at the screen door, not knowing what the situation inside might be. Clearly the doctor was still with Waine so he didn't want to interrupt.

Russ knocked ever so lightly, thinking he could turn and run any second. To his total surprise, Waine came to the door with a smile on his face and a pretty good gait for a man who needed help walking a few steps only a couple of hours ago. It seemed to Russ that whatever it was that had traumatized Waine had passed. Russ wasn't sure what to say.

Waine opened the door and came outside. "Hello, Russ. Why don't we sit out here on the deck?"

Doctor Legault followed Waine onto the now very-crowded deck. "Good to see you again. I'm not staying, Russ; I have left notes and some phone numbers where you can reach me over the next few days. Waine is going to review this with Denis when Denis comes back."

Turning to Waine, the doctor said, "I want you to review these notes about everything you and I discussed as soon as your brother gets back. Is that clear?"

Waine replied with a goofy smile and a sharp salute.

"Waine, nothing here to joke about. If I have to return again, other than as a guest, I mean, I will bring an ambulance with me and you will be taken to Nova Scotia's Mental Health facility in Halifax. That's not a threat, Waine. It's my diagnosis of how close you are to breaking down again if you don't take your meds even when you're feeling better. As I explained, the reason you were feeling well earlier was that you were taking your medication. It's the meds that are helping so do not...do *not*...stop taking them. And do not alter the dosage either. Got that?"

"I have, Doctor Legault, and I apologize for trying to lighten the mood. I do know how fragile my health is and I will review everything with Denis when he comes back".

As Russ got up to leave, the doctor said, "Russ, thank you for being a friend to these two new friends of mine. And thanks to your wife, also. Carol sat with Waine while I drove up the line a bit to pick up his prescription. I believe you slept through that part of our visit, Waine, but that's okay."

"Okay," Waine echoed.

"Russ," the doctor said, "I hate to keep you, but can you tell us how Denis got on with the wee one?"

"Yes, of course. Waine, your brother is with Lee on the beach. The boy is a whirlwind. He's damn smart too. He pointed out that his skin colour is like his Uncle's and I know that made Denis very proud. Lots of tears, but they're all good tears. Waine, Lee does call Paradise his mother, but he also speaks of your sister. I'm sorry for your loss. And with that I will take my leave."

Russ couldn't get out of there fast enough. Emotions weren't his favourite thing and he felt he was about to cry. No one needed to see that!

But he had to say one last thing from the ground. "Waine, I have a feeling you and Denis won't be ready to leave when your two weeks are up, so come and see me. I've got an idea about how you could stay here for longer, much longer. At a lower rate, too. We'll talk, okay?"

Doctor Legault hugged his patient and took his leave. Driving along Cape St Mary road he recognized the car heading toward him. He slammed on the brakes in his rental and stopped without even pulling to the side of the road. Thomas stopped, too, and Denis rolled down the back-seat window.

Doctor Legault brought Denis up to date about the new medication. "I hid the meds in the back of the pillowcase on your bed. Just as a precaution, you understand. Please give Waine his next does at six this evening."

"Doctor, should I keep control of my brother's medication these days?" Denis was a bit panicked about the current situation especially with the doctor clearly driving away.

"Not just 'these days' Denis, but always." Looking past Thomas, he went on. "I don't believe I have met this handsome young man..."

"I'm not a man." Not for the first time today Lee proceeded to check out his fingers on one hand and hold up four. "See. I'm four."

"You're a very smart four year old. I bet you enjoyed meeting your uncle. Did did he tell you he has another uncle for you to meet?"

Lee seemed to look at his dad in confusion with that last statement, so the doctor decided it was time he moved on. "Be gentle with your brother, Denis. But he's anxiously waiting for your return, so don't let me keep you one more minute. I told him Lee would most likely return with you and that brought the first smile I've been able to coax out of him. He's got all of my numbers so please do keep in touch...as a friend, I mean."

In a moment everyone was back in their cars and en route in different directions.

51: *Not* your son

Lee was the first out of the car. "Two uncles? What? You both look...kind...kind of like when I look at myself in the mirror and see another me. But this isn't a mirror so I don't get it."

And with that Lee went to his sister and asked if she would take him to the beach. "Because I wasn't done running, Hope. Will you take me?"

"No, Lee, we're visiting with Uncle Denis and he was trying to introduce you to his brother. That's your Uncle Waine sitting in the chair, and I believe he is very anxious to meet you, so come with me and we will try this again."

Taking her brother's hand, Hope tentatively walked toward Waine. Her parents had explained that Waine's mental health was very fragile but Hope wasn't totally sure what that even meant. She would ask her mom later, but it was time to make introductions.

"Waine, hi, my name is Hope and I'm Lee's big sister. Lee, this is your Uncle Waine. He came here with his brother, Denis, to get to know you. Waine and Denis didn't know your mommy had to go to heaven until just a few days ago. Well, maybe a week or two ago, but that doesn't matter."

She took a deep breath and said, "Do you have any questions, Lee?" Hope knew Lee's questions might be about anything...anything at all.

Lee surprised everyone. It was as if he knew his Uncle Waine was a bit fragile. He walked over to stand directly in front of Waine, and asked, "Uncle Waine, do you want me to sit on your lap? Would that cheer you up? It cheered my other uncle up when I sat on his lap, but then he cried. You must have been in a time-out since you had to stay here and couldn't come to the beach with us. I sure do know what that feels like."

Everyone; Thomas, Paradise, Hope and Uncle Denis were in awe of this four-year old who single-handedly defused the situation. And he wasn't quite finished. "Uncle Waine, do you ever get a time-out when you didn't do *anything* wrong? That happens to me and it's the worst. I hate that. Do you hate it, too?"

Everyone could see the smile on Waine's face. "Son, you—"

"Oh. My. God. I am *not* your son. Why does everyone keep calling me that?" Lee spoke so quickly it was hard to keep up with his thoughts. "Only mommy and daddy, and my other mommy but she's in heaven, can call me that because, well, just because."

Turning to Hope, Lee whispered, "I forgot to be quiet and not interrupt."

"Don't tell me. Tell your Uncle Waine you're sorry. He's the one you interrupted."

Hope turned Lee around so he could apologize with his dark eyes looking directly into his uncle's dark eyes.

"Sorry, Uncle Waine, I can't say one single word, even when grown up people go on and on and on. I just have to listen and listen."

"Good enough," Paradise said, trying to move things forward.

Thomas decided to wade in. "Waine, we haven't been properly introduced, I'm Thomas and Paradise is my wife. Before we moved here, the four of us piled into our little car and tried for a week to find Wikolia's family. I don't know why we couldn't find you, and I'm so sorry about Wikolia's death. I know you loved your sister very much."

Thinking he would add a bit of levity, Thomas added, "And, don't forget, I watched your sister tackle both of you and take you down. Didn't your mother and Wikolia take the two of you to the pavement later on the same day? I've got that right haven't I?"

Thomas saw everyone smile. Everyone except Lee, and Thomas could see his young mind at work.

"Wait! *Wait.* Did my mother beat you up? That's so cool, right, Hope?"

And *just like that*, Paradise thought, Lee helped everyone heal a bit more and feel a bit closer to each other.

"Hey, can I sleep here tonight? Can I, mom? Can I, dad?"

"Not tonight, son, but maybe in a few more days if that's okay with your uncles." Thomas wanted to wrap things up since Denis was anxious to speak with his brother alone.

~

When the others had left, Denis studied his brother. He seemed more like himself. Denis could see that just one brief visit with Lee had helped Waine immensely so more of the same would be on the agenda for tomorrow and for many tomorrows after that.

Denis made a mental note to follow up with Russ about the availability of their cottage for longer than two weeks. They would have to see if there was perhaps a smaller cottage, something not quite as expensive. They could afford it for two weeks, but that would be their limit as far as money went. They had nothing to get home to, so anything was possible if they could find a bit of work.

Denis would see what Waine felt like doing once Waine was on his new meds. He looked like he was feeling much better now that they had arrived in this beautiful part of the world. They had already agreed that Cape St Mary felt like Paradise, though they didn't use 'Paradise" as a description of the Cape in front of anyone outside of their little cottage.

52: Barely a whisper

Len was feeling beaten down and beaten up. He was dreading his morning meeting with Jalen and had just put in a tough shift. Concentration was impossible.

Lenny knew if he confused facts or deviated from the truth he'd be lost. Jalen would be upset, too. But he was having a rough time remembering all the facts and that had been weighing heavy on Len's shoulders as he navigated through the fog.

"Jalen," Lenny said with a nod to his Lieutenant Commander (always Jalen when they were on the inside), "you wanted to see me?"

Lenny sat down on one of the two red leather chairs in the 'big' office and he knew Jalen would sit beside him.

"In a word, *Lenny*, as she calls you, I want to speak with you about one Miss Bonde." Jalen was surprised when Len appeared stunned by the singular agenda item. He was certain Bonde would have run directly from his office to the man she called *her Lenny.*

A couple of weeks had passed with Len seeming to have had a number of meetings outside of the warehouse so they hadn't been able to schedule a meeting earlier. Jalen assumed all meetings had been with Len's handlers working to get him into the witness protection program. Maybe Len would tell him how all that was working for him this time. If he decided not to share, that was okay, too.

But it was not like Len to avoid a meeting with his employer. Jalen couldn't think of any meeting in the past that Len didn't quickly agree to and then attend. Maybe there was more to this relationship than he realized.

"Did Bonde not go directly to you a few weeks ago, all proud of herself for tattling on you because you made a long distance call to Paradise? I think she was jealous, to be honest, but I did tell her I would speak with you. Consider that done…and do not give me any details. I hope you have learned by now that I do not want to know about Bonde's love life—or yours in fact." Jalen was smiling so Lenny relaxed.

"Jalen, believe me, Bonde is the least of my worries. I wish she was all I had on my mind"

"Spit it out, son."

"I've got a bit of bad news."

"If you're trying to scare me, Len…" Jalen had to pause and check his own emotions. He feared something bad was about to be on the table. "Sorry about that, son, I think I had something in my throat so I needed a drink of water…now, where were we?"

It was barely a whisper. Jalen didn't see it coming.

"Lung cancer."

Len hung his head to hide the fact that he was crying. Trying to lighten things, he added, "Bet you never thought you would see tears running down my ugly face."

Jalen didn't know what to say or how to say it. "Are you sure of this, Len?"

He was now the one whispering and that made Len cry even more. Imagine, reducing his Lieutenant Commander to a whisper.

"Yes. I'm sure." Len couldn't continue until he, one more time, got control of his emotions. "I thought telling you would be easier. I guess it's the first time I've said the words, 'lung cancer' aloud since leaving the office of my oncologist."

Jalen slowly stood up and left his office for a minute or two, thinking Len needed time to compose himself. He grabbed coffee for both men and, taking a very deep breath, walked back into his office.

This time, the Lieutenant Commander sat behind his desk and motioned for Len to sit across from him. Jalen thought it would be easier for both men this way. Initially, when Jalen had thought they were meeting to discuss Bonde he hadn't wanted to make eye contact with Len.

Jalen didn't have much knowledge about lung cancer, but he did know his way around an oncologist's office. He knew what questions to ask when the patient's mind goes blank. Jalen had a feeling he would be learning more than a bit about lung cancer before this day was over.

"Len, I want to know everything, but if you need that discussion to begin a couple of hours from now that's okay with me. So, which is it? Do you need to get away from me or are you good to go?"

"Good to go."

"You don't sound like you mean that, especially since three words are all you have given me."

"Technically, five words if you count 'lung cancer', and for the re-cord, I'm allowed to make fun of cancer but you're not."

"That won't be a problem," Jalen said. "Some things are making sense to me now, son. I assumed you were off site meeting with your WPP handlers but now I'm thinking you've been meeting with medical people. Good ones, I hope. Experts, ideally, so, can I ask you to fill me in? Please begin at the very beginning of what has now turned into a cancer diagnosis."

"I guess I haven't been feeling all that well for a while. I didn't see it coming since I have pretty much never been ill in my life. Lots of broken bones, of course, but as you well know, my broken bones were never because of ill health."

"Okay, so you haven't been feeling well. What happened next?" Jalen was nervous for his young friend.

"I went to my regular doctor and he suggested I didn't look well in addition to not feeling well. He ordered some blood tests and then he sent me for an immediate x-ray. It was only one day later when the doctor's office called saying I was to have a cat-scan later that day and that the doctor would then be in touch as soon as he received the results." Len paused to drink a bit of his coffee.

"Take you time, son. Take your time."

"Jalen, I have to say I figured I was sick, but I didn't think I was cancer-sick. When my doctor called, he said something like, 'Len I won't know with absolute certainty about this until I send you for a biopsy, but I'm 99% confident in saying you have lung cancer.' He told me I have a large mass on the bottom inside corner of my left lung. The last thing Doctor Harvey said was, 'I want an oncologist to have a look at your biopsy so we can determine what stage of cancer we are dealing with. Only then can we develop a plan to treat you.' The only other thing he told me, Jalen, was that I would receive a call about a date for my biopsy before day's end today. That's all I've got."

"I'd like to help you, son. Will you let me do that?"

"Can you wave your magic wand and make cancer go away?"

"I'm not kidding, and don't cast aside my organizational skills compared to...let's say *your* organizational skills."

"What is it you think you would be able to do, Jalen? How could you help me?"

"I haven't got that figured out yet, Len, but for now I've got the name of a Doctor Harvey on your file, and that's it. Is Doctor Harvey still your doctor?"

"Yes."

"Do you have the name of the Oncologist? I want to do a bit of research on everyone on your medical team. I will promise you this, young man: I have the means, as does 2.0, as does Hawaii 5.0 to secure the best-possible treatment course for you. You let me know when it's time to take you off the job while you fight this beast. Got that?"

"Roger that, Jalen. Thank you."

That's all Len could manage to say. He made a fast exit back to his 2.0 personal quarters.

53: The boys bond

Len hadn't been back in his quarters for more than ten minutes when Jalen appeared at his door. "Grab your coat, son. You and I are going out on the town...my treat."

He stopped there, as it seemed he had literally shocked or frightened Len. "Sorry, Len, I should have knocked or said something before raising my voice. How does a big steak sound to you?"

"It sounds like you have forgotten that I go on shift in about 2.5 hours. Imagine if Bonde arrives at work only to see me show up hours later with a full belly and all liquored up. One way or another, she might kill me"

"All taken care of, son. I called Bonde and gave her the night off. I told her that you and I have a few off-site things to attend to and that you would give her all the details tomorrow night. Bonde was all over the place and now I see that she was trying to tell me something without telling me anything. She knows about your cancer diagnosis, I assume, and in that phone call she demonstrated her loyalty to you. Impressive. However, she began rapid-firing questions at me so I gently disconnected her. And," Jalen added, "I can only say that it felt good."

"Chicken," Len said.

"Absolutely, and imagine how thrilled, dare I say excited, Bonde will be to see you at the beginning of your midnight shift tomorrow night. Now, grab your coat and let's get out of here before she calls you to find out why she got a night off."

Both men laughed out loud when Len's phone rang at exactly that instant. He didn't pick it up, but he looked forward to listening to Bonde's message later.

Paradise d'Entremont, Private Investigator

54: *No* friends

The foursome loved spending time together. 'The Kids,' as both Pops and Eugenie called Wilmot and Marie, had been the first to suggest they get together.

"Look down near the wharf, Wilmot, way down at the end of the beach. It's Pops and Eugenie just arriving at Mavillette and they're headed our way. We have met them on the beach so many times…I think we should walk together more often than we do now. What do you think?"

"I don't know, Marie. I love it just the two and now three of us walking the beach twice a day. We talk about so many things. It's not as if we need more friends, is it? Would Rescuee appreciate the change? She has just gotten used to walking between the two of us so maybe we're okay for now?"

"More friends? *More friends*? I hate to break it to you, Wilmot, but we have *no* friends at all. Family members are automatically friends in our world and even family is not much more than the oc-cupants over at 548 Cape St Mary Road—"

A seemingly-angry Wilmot interrupted. "What in God's good name are you talking about, Marie? Of course we have friends. We have tons of friends."

"Name one."

"Actually, I can name two. The two Hawaiian boys over in Cabin #3 are my friends. My good friends."

"Sorry, my love, I didn't realize that. What are there names, Wilmot? Rumour has it they may be moving here. Have they shared that with you? I know you have mentioned them, but, hon-estly, I didn't realize you had become friends. I'm really happy to hear this and I hope to meet them soon myself."

"Well, I guess I should say I have wanted to get to know them better and become friends. They came all the way over here to meet little Lee, who is somehow connected to the family."

"Do we see them on the beach when we are there? I'm not sure I've ever seen them. Maybe they're runners?"

"When you see them, Marie, you'll realize where my confidence comes from when I say I would bet my life they're not runners. Hard core body builders *maybe,* but I'm not so sure they run any-where."

"Do Pops and Eugenie know them?" Marie was anxious to know more about the Cape View Two.

"Well, let's ask them since they are almost face-to-face with us. In the fog this morning it's a bit hard to tell until we smack into them, so be careful."

Wilmot was glad to have gotten away with his little non-truth about being friends with the cabin #3 occupants.

When the two became four, Eugenie spoke first. "Pops and I have tried to confirm, all the way from the wharf where our walk began, if it was the two of you walking our way. Fog's some thick this morning. Haven't seen it like this in ages."

Wilmot wanted to take control of the conversation, at least for a minute or two, but he wasn't fast enough. Marie had more to say.

"Eugenie, do you and Pops know the two boys who checked in last week over at the Cape View? Wilmot tells me they're brothers and they're in cabin #3, but that seems to be all he can tell me."

"Oh, my good Lord, this is such a great story, Marie. Here, you walk with me and let the men walk behind us...as it should be." Eugenie laughed at her own joke, but she and Pops did that a lot and she had to try hard to stay ahead of him.

"There will be no end to this conversation taking place right in front of us, Pops," Wilmot said. "Look at the two of them already with their heads together. And, it looks like my wife is doing all the talking at the moment."

Pops smiled as he tried to hear what was being discussed. "Don't you worry, my friend. My wife will have her say. She always has something to say and I love it. I've got me one strong woman."

Wilmot hadn't heard one word after 'my friend.' He was right in his thinking that he does have, at the very least, *one friend* and he would make sure Marie knew it, too!

Eugenie spoke softly and with the howl of the wind Marie had some difficulty hearing what she was saying, but it was a good story indeed. "As I understand it, and I don't have this first hand, the brothers' names are Denis and Waine. That much I can say is 100% accurate. Denis seems to be the one in charge. I hear Waine has some sort of a disability, although I haven't seen it myself, but there you have it."

As Eugenie drew breath to continue, Marie jumped in. She had a bad habit of doing that, Eugenie thought. The last time Marie had interrupted her, Eugenie had let it go, but today would be different.

"Are Denis and Waine staying long? Russ was telling me, just before they arrived, that the residents in cabin #3 were booked for two full weeks."

Marie seemed awfully sure of this, Eugenie thought. "As I was saying—"

"I'm so sorry Eugenie, I interrupted you."

"And you did it again, my dear, so I will ask you to please let me finish. I'm almost done anyway." Eugenie knew that sounded a bit harsh and she was sorry she had said it, but not sorry enough to admit it.

"It seems, and this may not be true at all, that that beautiful little boy, Lee, is the son of one of the two men. I can tell you I near fainted when I heard that. I also heard a totally different version, that Lee is their nephew. One of those two stories must be true, I figure."

Suddenly, Marie had an idea. She didn't have time to talk it over with Wilmot but she didn't think he would mind. "Eugenie, I would like to invite you and Pops over for dinner one of these nights, and let's invite Denis and Waine to join us. I bet they don't get too many home-cooked meals the way they are living right now, so they would likely appreciate the invite."

"Just tell me when and what Pops and I can bring to add to the meal. Should we invite the two men or do you and Wilmot want to do that?"

"Oh, Wilmot so badly wants to be friends with Denis and Waine, so let's leave that job for him, if that's okay with you." Marie was already thinking of what she would put on her list the second she got back home and grabbed her pen and paper. "Today's Wednesday so let's say Saturday around 5 pm. That gives me a few days to shop and prepare a couple of things ahead of time. Eugenie, would you be okay with bringing dessert...anything you want as long as it has chocolate in it! The more chocolate the better. Honestly if you want to purchase something rather than making it you won't hurt my feelings at all. I can't make dessert to save my soul. Oh my God, I apologize for my poor choice of words. I'm prone to believing my soul will be saved regardless of how much chocolate I consume. However, I bow to you, the expert in all-things about our post-life life."

When Eugenie was able to stop laughing, something she was forbidden to do while her only home was a convent, she said, "I'm no longer a nun, as you have most likely figured out since I am married to Pops. I am a practising Catholic, though, and I don't care much for swearing, so I will ask you to tuck that little nugget of information away in your head and bring it with you on Saturday. Can you do that for this old nun turned wife?"

Eugenie was laughing so Marie thought she would end the conversation and pick it up again tomorrow. "Roger that, as Paradise or Hope would say. Roger that."

Then she stopped in her tracks. "Oh no. Until you said 'Paradise' I didn't give it a moment's thought, but think about it...we can't have a dinner party and not invite Paradise and Thomas. Can we? It just doesn't seem right to me." Eugenie was certain Pops would want them to be included in something as intimate as a pre-planned dinner party.

Marie didn't disagree but facts were facts. "Have you seen my home, Eugenie? It's a lovely 'A' framed cottage with plenty of room for one or two. We've added four more to make six and you want to add another two? Really?"

Eugenie had an idea. "Let's talk mid-morning tomorrow. I have an idea that might work, but trust me until tomorrow and I'll fill you in then. Should we try saying bye for now one more time?"

"Roger that," Marie said. "But, don't take too long in getting back to me. I am mentally working on my grocery list as we speak."

55: Hawaiian boys

Cabin #3 was a favourite destination now, not only for Denis and Waine but for Lee and Hope in particular. Even Paradise and Thomas dropped in now and again. Things were looking up for the brothers from Honolulu.

"Good morning, Waine," Denis said. "You beat me to the kitchen this morning. What time did you get up?"

Denis could see that Waine had already showered and dressed. He hadn't really been out of bed for the better part of a week and none of that 'mental health slip' was visible to the eye, unless you were his brother and had all the facts.

"I woke up feeling great for the first morning in a long time, but it was only 6 am. I tried going back to sleep and couldn't, so thought I would get up and clean my room and get a start on making coffee. I have already been over to Russ and Carol's to pick up a couple of muffins and I told them we might be back for coffee before the 'kitchen' shut down for the day. They were really happy to see me. I was almost embarrassed. How bloody long have I been my own prisoner in my bedroom? Black coffee for you...here you go. Maybe I'll open a coffee shop. Wasn't hard to make at all." Waine was on a roll.

Denis winced as he took a sip of his brother's coffee. "Waine, I love you, man, but there is a reason we have our coffee with Carol and Russ. Have you tasted this? And to answer your question, you've been in bed for almost a week, but that's all behind you now. I'm so proud just seeing you this morning, honest to God, man."

The boys hugged it out!

"I haven't had even one cup of coffee this morning," Waine said.

"I was waiting for you to get up. It can't be that bad."

Denis poured a coffee and set it in front of him with a smile on his face. He wanted Waine to realize he wasn't mad at him. "Go ahead. Drink it. I challenge you, bro. If you can drink it, I will, too. So come on, bottom's up."

Waine took a large gulp of his coffee. He stood up and turned away from Denis so he could keep the face he was making to himself. It really wasn't coffee at all.

When he had managed to swallow he said, "Why don't I head over for a coffee and you can meet me there."

Denis hugged his brother again. "Actually, I wanted to talk with you about something before we go over. Let me grab a quick shower, get dressed and we'll head out. I'll be under ten minutes, I promise."

"That's fine with me. Don't rush. I still have more packing to do and now that I have my suitcase out, and in the middle of my bed, I might as well finish. Why did we bring so much for two weeks?"

"Maybe we were planning to stay longer than two weeks. Maybe we didn't stop to think how wonderful it would be to find and get to know Lee. Maybe we didn't realize this truly is paradise...even better than our homeland, although we have not experienced this 'winter' they talk about yet. How bad can winter be? That's what I want to discuss, so think about that. I'll be right back."

Waine could hear the shower turn on seconds after Denis spoke so he knew he really was going to be fast. He slowly walked into his room and sat wondering what he had missed over the last week and a bit. Denis sure was good to him.

The last thing Denis had said as Waine was heading to bed the previous night was, "By the time you wake up tomorrow morning, little brother, this last change in your medications Doctor Legault prescribed should have totally kicked in. The doctor said it would *definitely* be well into your system within one week. Tomorrow is going to be all about you, so sleep well and dream about Mavillette beach!"

True to his word Denis, came out of his room in full flight. "It's been nine minutes and I need coffee. I need real coffee. I need good coffee…"

"Okay, I get it. I won't try to make your precious coffee again. I thought you wanted us to sit and talk about something before we headed out. So, are we going or are we staying? For God sake, don't confuse me, Denis."

Denis could see that Waine was joking a bit and that was a very good sign related to his mental health. "Briefly, because I do need coffee, Russ has dropped in to check on you a few times. He said as he was leaving one day that if we decided to stick around for a while he could give us the long-term rate for our cabin and we could also earn a bit of money helping him out around here, if that was of interest to us."

Waine's first comment was, 'Do you want to stay?"

"Yes, I do. Can I ask you the same question, Waine?"

"Yes. I would love to stick around and, honestly, we have nothing pulling us back to Hawaii anytime soon."

That made Denis very happy.

"Face it, brother," Waine went on, "we are two fat, out of shape, and unemployed fight-club champions, and given that we have made the decision to change careers we can stay here forever. And, I should add that in my case we can add mental health issues to the mix." Isn't that about it in a nutshell?"

Waine was trying to throw in a bit of humour at his own expense. *The old Waine*, Denis thought.

Denis was on the move but he did have one more comment. "Oh, and I am *not* fat. I do seem to be a few pounds heavier than when we arrived, but that does not make me fat. Got that?"

"A *few* pounds heavier?"

"Okay maybe *several* pounds heavier but I'm *not* fat. Got that?"

Lagging a bit behind, Waine thought he would simply use one of Hope's words. It seemed to work well for her. "Sure."

56: Authentic boxing gloves

Russ had a huge smile on his face as he held the office door open for Denis and Waine. He hadn't seen much of Waine during their first week at the Cape View and he was thrilled to see them both arriving for their continental breakfast.

Behind him, Carol inhaled sharply and whispered, "Look at them side by side. My God, Russ, they could be twins!"

Russ replied just seconds before greeting his guests, "They have not presented themselves as twins, but always used the term brothers, so let's let them bring this up in their own time."

Carol got the message loud and clear.

During their first week in the Cape, Denis had gotten into the habit of picking up coffee and muffins, or whatever Carol had happened to make, and taking everything back to #3. Everyone in the community knew of the brothers and they were all pulling for Waine to be well enough to enjoy the beach and the sunshine.

Even the fog was of interest, because the heaviest fog-laden days were so often a topic of conversation and both Denis and Waine were anxious to experience it themselves. Even on a good day, bright, sunny and warm, you could still hear someone say, "Yes, it's all perfect today. But...did you *even see* the thick fog yesterday and the day before?"

'Fog stories' were often bedtime chatter between Waine and Denis. It was always Denis sharing the stories because, of course, Waine had yet to visit Mavillette beach.

"Waine, I am so happy to see you this morning. Come on in, Carol and I have both missed you."

"So, what am I...chopped liver?" Denis was enjoying himself for the first time in a few days. He was actually smiling as Carol gave him a wink.

She was happy for both of their guests.

"Come over here and stop complaining,"Russ said while he poured coffee. All the other guests had come for coffee and break-fast and were off to the beach or wherever, so it was just the four of them. Both Russ and Carol sat with them.

"Oh, oh, have we done something wrong?" Denis said. "You never take the time to sit down with any of your guests."

Waine wanted to join in so he offered a playful theory. "Denis, if *we* have done anything wrong *you* are guilty as hell. I've been in bed for a week so they can't make anything stick to me."

It wasn't lost on anyone that hearing Waine create a joke at his own expense made this day a little bit brighter.

Russ dove into the business part of the morning. "Denis, Waine, both Carol and I have thoroughly enjoyed having you here with us. We realize your two weeks ends tomorrow. We also know you have a young family member living in the Cape and he very much enjoys his daily visits with you. As Lee tells the story to his parents, you are going to give him boxing lessons *and* you're giving him a pair of boxing gloves. Good luck with finding boxing gloves around here! He also calls you his "fat Uncles," but I won't touch that one."

Russ was enjoying this so much. He had already checked all local stores for boxing gloves and came up with not-a-one pair.

"You don't have to search beyond #3 to find the boxing gloves," Waine said. "We got them in the gift shop at the Flight Club in Hon-olulu...smallest pair they had in stock."

Waine was so happy they had made the purchase and equally happy that Lee seemed interested in learning to box. Before Waine and his brother became Fight Club Champions they had been Ama-teur Boxing Champions for the state of Hawaii. They had shared all of this information with Paradise and Thomas before bringing it up with Lee.

Thomas thought boxing lessons were a great idea. Paradise...not so much. She wouldn't stop it from happening, though.

Russ went on, "I'm thinking you need a bit more time with Lee: to walk the beach with him or teach him how to box—"

Waine was quick to interrupt. "In the name of the Lord, we are not *walkers*. On the beach or anywhere else. In fact, we brought up boxing with the hopes that we would be too busy with that to have to head to the beach for long walks."

"Waine's right," Denis said. "Before we would appear at the Fight Club, we would slowly jog while shadow boxing for at least three hours a day...thus we have no interest in it today."

"Okay, let me jump in here with a work and residential possibility for you both," Russ said. "Carol and I could use a bit of help with the workload we face seven days a week, so this isn't us creating work but rather sharing the load. If we hire and train both of you, this would give us the opportunity to work a bit less and go into town together now and then, which we never get to do. One of us has to be in the office at all times to answer phones and be available to our guests. We wouldn't leave you on your own overnight... not in the early days, anyway. How does this all sound so far?"

"If you want time to think about it that's okay too," Carol said.

The boys looked at each other and exchanged a message in their private language of facial expressions created years ago to send signals to each other at Fight Night. Then Denis shifted round to face Russ directly. "We like what we're hearing so far. Hard work is not something we have ever been afraid of. The cost of our cottage would be our biggest worry, so can we talk about that next?"

"We sure can. How does this sound?"

Russ had to consult his tiny notebook for some figures before he went on. "Carol and I are in total agreement that if you could each give us three hours a day, and that can be when the sun is *not* shining, if that is your preference, cabin #3 would be yours at no monthly cost...so you're basically working for the roof over your head. This offer stands for as many months as you care to call the Cape home."

Russ gave a nod to Carol and she jumped in. "All we ask is that you give us a bit of notice if you have to leave us. One more thing, I almost forgot...your three hours a day would be for five days a week. For the most part you would have all of your weekends off. That might be a detail we can work out once you're on our staff."

"Most likely we will leave when the snow covers the ground," Waine quipped. "And every day is the weekend for Denis and me, so we're good with whatever you want to do, right Denis?"

"One question before I can agree to your offer," Denis said. "Three hours a day for both of us sounds like nothing at all and we are terribly grateful. If one of us needed a day off, say for mental health reasons, could the other brother work the six hours on that particular day if trained on everything?"

"Absolutely," Carol said. She topped up coffee for both Denis and Waine.

"So, now that we have that settled," Russ said with a wide grin, "do we have a deal, gentlemen?"

"Roger that. Where do we sign?" Denis said. He was extremely proud of his brother for being part of the conversation. Russ and Carol would never believe the state Waine had been in for the last very long days. Waine seemed to like the idea of setting down roots at least for a few months and Denis felt this would be good for his brother's mental health.

"Does Lee know about the possibility of us staying?" Waine asked. *I hope the answer is 'no'*, a voice in his head whispered. With him being ill he hadn't gotten to really know Lee yet, and he was looking forward to that very much.

"No,' Carol replied. "We haven't discussed this with anyone until right now. The story will be yours to tell. I must admit there is lots of interest in the bachelors in #3, so remember to lock your door, boys."

Carol stood, approached Denis and Waine, and gave each a big hug. Russ followed with a 'welcome aboard' handshake and added, "If you think you would be more comfortable with me training you both at the same time we can do that. Anything to make things work best for you! We mean that."

Carol Ann Cole

57: Give it a rest

"Lieutenant Commander Jalen Lexis speaking, identify yourself."

"Gentle Jesus, do you men ever give it a rest? You sound like your head's about to blow and you've only just arrived at work, right? Isn't it a bit early to be pissed off with the world?"

"I would normally ask you, once again, to identify yourself, but that vulgar mouth gives you away. Bonde, I assume?"

Jalen had hoped that Bonde would look after Lenny if cancer managed to knock him down. With this in mind, he had decided to be a bit kinder to her even if he couldn't quite manage to like her. On the other hand, if he had to like Bonde to make Len feel better, he would do that, too.

A few weeks had passed with Len and Bonde working the night shift together, after which Bonde would go home and Len would go to his in-house quarters and sleep for a few hours and then get up and go for his treatment. He was finding cancer to be relentless, but he was, for now, prepared to give it his all. He had visions of being cancer free one day.

"Bonde, are you calling me on my private line simply to chat?"

"I'm barely keeping it together, Jalen, and Len is sitting right beside me. We're at my place. He has asked me to call you, so please don't make this too hard on me."

"Done."

"Jalen, it's me, Len. Bonde came with me to meet my oncologist today. No indication yet if treatment is working, but the good doctor reminded me I'm in this for the long haul. That's not all I learned, but I need to stop talking and regulate my breathing. Bonde, will you take over for me?"

There was a bit of chat Jalen couldn't catch, and then Bonde was back on the phone. "Jalen, I am going to try to do my best to say what I'm saying with no more swearing. Lenny's oncologist, Doctor Dea, who is a lovely lady by the way, talked with Lenny about her concern with him working nights and some days and going directly from a twelve hour shift to the hospital for a treatment. She feels treatments are not as successful if the patient is bone tired and having to drag himself to the hospital."

"Bonde, stop with the details and tell me what you and Len need. And is he okay as he sits beside you concentrating on his breathing?" Clearly Len's cancer was worse than Jalen assumed.

"He's nodding, Jalen, and I'll get right to the point...why we are calling you, I mean. To take better care of Lenny, we would like to move him from the warehouse to my apartment. Doctor Dea said he should take a few weeks off work so we can get him sleeping at night and up and out of bed for the day. I will stay on nights and will try very hard to do Lenny's job as well as mine, so maybe you won't have to dock him for the time he has to be off work. Doctor Dea said that Lenny must battle this cancer beast twenty-four hours every damn day. Jalen, I'm embarrassed to admit this but I'm not in the financial position to take time off work."

There was barely a pause. "There will be no docking of your pay, Len. And, Bonde, while I appreciate your offer, I would rather you take time off work as well to care for Len. Get yourself on the same schedule so you can sleep at the same time. I won't be docking your pay either. Let's take this one month at a time and, simply put, I don't want to see either of you at the warehouse."

Len spoke next and with some degree of difficulty. Jalen wondered if it was more than the cancer. He seemed to be crying. "Jalen, thanks from both of us. Believe it or not, Bonde started crying first and I followed. I do need a few personal things from my quarters, so perhaps Bonde could pick them up later today...if she stops bawling..."

"Tell me what you need, son, and I will deliver everything mid afternoon. Bonde, I have your address on file so I can find my way to your apartment. Is there anything you need from here, from the grocery store, from the wine store? Make a list and call my secretary with it before lunchtime."

"Jalen, you have made our lives much easier to navigate, for the next month at least. Len is going to beat this f...sorry this cruel disease. You are welcome here any time Jalen, and I'll even give you boys a bit of alone time, if you want it. I know how men like their alone time! If you're coming mid-afternoon you are welcome to stay for dinner. It's a fact that I whip up gourmet meals and even Len can testify to this. For the record, Lenny is nodding and giving me the thumbs up sign."

"If I'm staying for dinner I'm bringing dinner with me, so everything is settled. See you this afternoon." With that, Jalen hung up. Jalen hung up on everyone. The words *bye* or *good bye* or even *later* were not in his memory bank. Jalen didn't think it was anyone's business how he chose to end all phone calls.

58: Family ties

"Wilmot and Marie, I'm so glad you're here. Come on in. I thought perhaps we should put your Rappie pie in the warming oven, correct? Marie, can you remind me what's in this dish? I've only had it once."

Paradise was truly interested. So many individuals, locals in the area, speak of Rappie pie at every meal.

"I'm happy to share, Paradise. This Rapure, en Français, is made of grated potato, onion and chicken. I also made a broth to be poured over individual servings to everyone's liking. I doubled the receipt when it was just going to be Pops and Eugenie joining Wilmot and me. I tripled the receipt when I learned Denis and Waine would join the party and that everything would move to your home because the party has quickly outgrown our little cottage. I sure don't mind us coming here instead."

Marie stepped closer and whispered, "Even if we all chip in with the cleanup, there will be work for you to do long after we have all returned to our homes with full stomachs."

"We are more than happy to host everyone. I think we are all interested in Denis and Waine and this is a great way to sit down and, over drinks and dinner, get to know each other better. And we get to let the boys know how delighted we are to have them with us long after their two-week vacation was to be over. Marie, why don't you join the men in the living room? I see more guests arriving, so I'll get the door."

Paradise rushed to open the door. "Come in. Come in and welcome. Pops and Eugenie, you've both been here a million times, so just make yourselves comfortable in the living room. Pops, would you do me a favour? Make sure everyone has something to drink and a chair to sit on."

"Done," Pops replied.

Paradise turned to speak with Denis and Waine, who had arrived behind Pops and Eugene, and now stood in the open doorway "Welcome to our home, gentlemen. Come on in. I would very much like to introduce both of you to everyone myself. I realize most of our guests know you, but I would like to tell them about our family ties. Is that okay with you?"

The boys both started talking at the same time. Then Denis took over and said, "Paradise, that would be wonderful. To be honest, we are never sure how to explain our connection to your family, so having you cover that for us will make our visit more comfortable. Right, Waine?"

"Lead the way," Waine said, already showing a bit of emotion. He blamed it on the medication.

"Paradise, perhaps you could put a cold beer in our hands before you introduce us," Denis added with a laugh that filled the room. "Beer always helps our nerves settle."

"I can do better than that. Look, right here in the mudroom fridge. You can pick your favourite beer and have it in hand before we go through the kitchen and into the living room to be with our guests. In fact, I think I'll join you, so I'll have whatever you're having."

Denis opened three bottles of beer and handed one to his brother and another to their hostess. "Cheers, all. Let's do this."

"Uncle Denis! Uncle Waine!" Lee shouted as he ran full-on toward his uncles.

Clearly the trio had done this before, or had certainly practised for today. The uncles turned facing each other with only a bit of space between them and all four hands on alert and ready to catch their nephew as he jumped easily into a near-by chair and flung himself towards a safe family catch.

Applause all around. Then Paradise jumped in. "I'm not sure where you learned to do that, Lee, but we do *not* jump on the furniture in the house. You understand that, right?"

She wasn't displeased at all, really. Everyone was smiling, but she could see by the looks on some of the faces that an explanation would be necessary, given how easily Lee had referred to Denis and Waine as his uncles.

Lee wanted to debate this. "I know about chair jumping, but I thought it would be okay for this special occasion and we practised so many times over at the Cape. It was cool, right, mommy? And it's a very special occasion, right?"

Knowing she could not compete with the logic of a five-year-old in front of guests Paradise decided she might be better off if she joined in. "It was very cool, Lee. Now, you and your sister have things to do for our little party and I believe Hope is already in the kitchen, so off you go, please."

"In the *kitchen*? That's funny, mommy."

With Lee's last comment Eugenie was exchanging looks with Marie. Now they were certain that Paradise was this little boy's mother.

"Lee, not another word. Go and find your sister."

Hope to the rescue. "Lee I need your help so giddy-up."

Hope wasn't a fan of the expression but it worked with Lee every time. He gaily galloped to her side.

"If I could have everyone's attention," Paradise began as she moved to stand between the two men. "Over the past few weeks you have all met Denis and Waine, or at least you have seen them around. And you know their temporary home is cabin #3. Am I right?"

Paradise had everyone's attention. Some were leaning in to ensure they heard every word.

"There is much more to share. I know there has been all kinds of gossip. Yes, I did hear the rumour that I had given birth to Lee myself, I can confirm that is not the case. He calls me mommy, I know, and to his young mind I am his mother. We speak openly about his birth mother and we always will."

She turned to Thomas "Do you want to jump in at this stage?"

"Yes, that sounded a bit confusing at the end of what Paradise had to say but I can easily clear things up. Prior to Paradise joining Hope and me in Hawaii, I was in a long-term relationship with a lovely lady, Wikolia Lee. Denis and Waine are Wikolia's brothers and they arrived to meet and get to know their nephew and—"

Denis interrupted, "And we are so grateful for the warm welcome you gave us, Paradise and Thomas. All of you, actually."

Waine said, "I have to interrupted, Denis, because I know where you were going and I want to join in and thank everyone for being so kind, so pleasant and so concerned when I didn't come out of #3 for almost a week. I'm much better now, to the extent anyone with a mental illness can be better. I'm good, is what I normally say, but I don't often mean it. Today, here with Lee and his family who have all taken Denis and me in as part of the family I mean it. *I am good.* We are both good. Additionally we are humbled, grateful and quite handsome, don't you think?"

Waine took another beer and was quite proud of himself. He didn't cry until he said both he and Denis were humbled, and then the floodgates opened.

Understanding how he felt, Denis moved to hug his brother before speaking again. "Thanks for that, brother. I'm forever proud of you. We're proud of our sister, Wikolia, too."

With the mention of their sister, Denis began to cry. "Our sister has died. I think that's all we will say at this point if you will allow. I understand this is meant to be a happy gathering, so I may have misspoke in sharing such a sad thing. We realize you-all will have questions...but not tonight."

"Well said, Denis." Thomas felt they should acknowledge the comments from the boys without adding anything more. They were always happy to speak of Wikolia, but there was more to come this evening and he wanted to keep the mood joyful and family focused.

Paradise said, "Hope and Lee will serve our meal tonight, but we have one more activity before food arrives and I think it's time to get that underway. Don't you agree Thomas?"

"I do," Thomas said as he looked directly at Paradise for longer than needed. "Can you find the kids for me? I think they're upstairs."

"I'm off to join the children for a minute or two. Everyone, make sure you have all you need. Thomas will be happy to serve you."

They thought they were pulling this off beautifully. But before Thomas could speak, Lee yelled from upstairs and as only a child could do. "Mommy, aren't you and daddy getting *marriaged* today? Why are Hope and I all dressed up and stuck upstairs?"

Paradise rushed upstairs hoping to catch Lee before he went on. He managed to get his new word out one more time. "Is there going to be a *marriaged* or not, Mommy?"

Everyone heard the closing of the bedroom door. Suddenly it was quiet upstairs. And, in fact, it was quiet downstairs as well.

59: Marriaged!

"It's all good, folks" Paradise said. "*Please, I beg you,* don't ask me any questions. I promise that everything will become clear in a-bout ten minutes, possibly less."

And, oh thank God, saved by the bell. The doorbell.

Thomas, smiling broadly, was on the way to open the door. He knew who it was. "Reverend Service, thank you so much for com-ing to conduct our marriage ceremony. I'll take you directly up-stairs since we are trying to keep all-things-wedding quiet until we actually begin. We were on track until our almost-five-year-old said too much."

Two minutes later, Thomas was dressed and ready to go. He met the children outside of their bedroom, knowing his bride was just inside. Having almost forgotten, he whispered through the door to Paradise, "Do we know if Pops can climb stairs, sweetheart?"

"I decided not to ask Pops ahead of time because I do know that Eugenie would feel left out if she didn't know about our wedding when Pops did. Could you ask Pops to come up to our room now, please? I'm ready, too, so as soon as Pops comes up the three of you should go downstairs."

"Yes, honey, we know the drill, so you just chill until Pops ar-rives. I can't wait to see you and make you my wife."

Thomas had thought of this day a million times and there were times he had been convinced it would never happen. *Finally* that day had arrived. He was almost as excited as Lee to be getting *mar-riaged* today.

"Pops?"

"Are you calling me, Thomas? Is everything okay?" Pops was a bit startled to learn that Thomas needed him for something.

"Everything is perfect. If you can do stairs, could you come up here for a second or two?"

"I can't take steps two at a time as I once did, but I'll have you know, young man, that I can make it from one floor to the next with no difficulty."

With that, Pops was on the upstairs landing looking at Thomas, who was in a tux and trying to hide someone who stood behind him. "Who are you hiding for heaven's sake, Thomas? Oh. My. God. as Hope would say. Reverend Service is that you?"

Pops extended his hand to Reverend Service. "Ah, now I know what's going on."

"Not another word please, Pops," Thomas said. "Paradise would like you to join her." He opened their bedroom door just wide enough for Pops to step inside.

The trio of Lee, Hope and Thomas walked downstairs to the living room as formally as they could, with interlocked arms and huge smiles.

"Told ya." Not a soul in the room had to wonder who had just spoken. Even Thomas relaxed a bit.

This time, Lee would speak with permission from his daddy. "Guess what? Me and Hope and mommy and daddy are gonna get *marriaged* right in this room before I have to eat my supper. Then I have to brush my teeth and go to bed. I always have to brush my teeth and I hate that. I'll be *marriaged* by the time I go to bed, right, Hope?"

"Yes, my little brother, you will be *marriaged* by then."

Hope couldn't contain her happiness for her parents. She picked Lee up and twirled him around until Thomas had to tell her to stop.

"Please don't encourage him, Hope. He's loving the limelight just a bit too much for my liking."

Thomas took his appointed place in the room. "Hope, I need you on one side of me and Lee, I need you on the other side. We are going to stand here with Reverend Service. Got it?"

"Yes, dad."

"Yes, daddy."

Upstairs, Pops went directly to Paradise and hugged her for so long she feared their guests might leave.

"Pops, I hope you will forgive me for not giving you any advance notice. I'll explain all of that and more another time. For now, will you walk me downstairs and down the imaginary aisle in the living room?"

"Paradise, first of all, you are a vision in your beautiful long wedding dress. It could be just my imagination but is it the same dress young Hope is wearing...in another colour?"

There was so much more Pops wanted to say, but words were not coming to him. He knew his emotions were all over the place. He knew this was exactly the way he had felt the day he and Eugenie got married in Halifax.

"Good eye, Pops. Nothing wrong with your vision. My dress is Ivory while Hope's is Brilliant Red."

"Full disclosure, I thought Hope had forgotten to put her fancy brand new party dress on and was heading to the top of the stairs in her brilliant new slip. And now, as I look at you wearing that same dress in that Ivory colour, yours also looks like a slip. Although now that I see the length you have chosen, I would call yours a gown. This is the current fashion statement, so I guess I have even more to learn."

He gave his head a shake. "Who am I kidding? It can be nothing but nerves that have me talking fashion! Paradise, you look beautiful and I am so happy for you...for all four of you."

Pops stepped back and watched in silence as Paradise put her boots on. *Boots? Wedding boots maybe?*

"I'm almost ready, Pops. Don't let me forget to pin this rose on your jacket. Everyone in the wedding party has one and we delivered a few downstairs as well...including one for Eugenie."

"You're the main event. I figure you can take all the time you need. Your mother and father would be so proud of the woman you are."

With that, Pops was in tears while Paradise was trying to keep it together.

"Pops, thank you for saying that. They have been on my mind all day. To lighten the mood and the conversation I will tell you we found these two dresses on sale in Yarmouth! We didn't even have to go up the line to shop." Paradise knew her nerves were keeping her from focusing on her wedding only minutes away and one floor below.

"Are you ready, Paradise?" Pops didn't much care either way since he couldn't stop crying, regardless of how hard he tried.

"I am, and thank you again for walking with me. I'm honoured to be on your arm today. And once you pass me over to Thomas, you can sit with Eugenie and enjoy yourself."

"That's all I need to know. Now, let's get you *marriaged,* as your son would say. I have to tell you, young lady, I sure am proud that you picked me for this honour. I had no idea."

~

Downstairs, Hope spoke to her brother from the other side of her dad. "Lee, are you supposed to do something with the roses you are carrying?"

"Yes," came the quiet reply.

After giving him a few seconds to remember his role, Hope stepped in. "Would you like me to give the roses to the ladies our mother wanted to have them?"

Thinking Lee might say 'no', Hope added, "Let's do it together, Lee. But we have to hurry before mommy walks down those steps, okay? You hold the roses and I'll go with you."

"I remember now so I'll say what I'm suppose to say to each one." Lee gave Hope his 'game on' look.

Elise saw the children walking towards her and she couldn't hold back the tears. She remembered Paradise's mom's wedding and how happy she was back then. She missed her best friend today. Paradise had invited Elise and suggested because this was a surprise to everyone she should arrive at a certain time and just go inside. No need to ring the doorbell or knock. A day like this was going to be a gift to everyone in this house.

As only a child could do, Lee lightened the mood with, "I'm getting *marriaged* today. Take one of these roses. I don't care which one."

Turning immediately to Hope, Lee asked, "Now which one do we go to?"

"Come with me, and remember we are *all* getting married today. It's not just about you. Mommy explained all of this to us, do you remember?"

"Yes."

"Lee, let's use our inside voice from now on. A wedding is supposed to be a gentle time. Let me hear your gentle voice?"

"Sure."

Lee had learned his one-word answer from Hope, so she accepted it and tried to hurry this part of the day up. She knew they should be finished and back on either side of their dad by now.

She took Lee's hand and put her other hand on his back to move him forward from his 'I'm not moving' stance. Finally they made it over to Eugenie, who received the second rose. Hope had to take the rose from Lee's firm grasp, but between her and Eugenie the passing of the rose took place.

Listening for the bedroom door upstairs to open, Hope decided they had time to give the final two roses out. She wasn't sure how this would play out, but as soon as Lee realized they were going to his uncles he almost toppled chairs to get to them.

Again Lee went off script, but his words were even better than the words he had practised so hard yesterday.

"Hi, Uncle Denis and Uncle Waine. Here, take these two roses. That's the end of them. You're getting roses but guess what, *they are not for you*. They are for my mother in heaven. She's dead so she can't come to my *marriaged*."

Lee was full of stories today, and everyone listened to his young voice "Mommy is coming down the stairs very soon so you and I need to hurry and stand beside daddy."

Hope tried in vain to move Lee on.

"No. I want to stay with my Uncles and I'm not moving."

Denis bent down to eye level with Lee and put their foreheads together. No one could hear what Denis whispered, but it was enough for Lee to rush over to his father's side.

Hope snuck away and back up the stairs so she could be with her mom and Pops.

"Ready. Set. Go. Mommy, come on down the stairs. I'm ready for real this time. I'm right beside daddy." Lee was not using his inside voice. "Wait. *Wait!* I forgot to say the most important thing. *Here comes the bride!*"

60: Wedding boots

Hope paused long enough to knock once before she entered the bedroom where Paradise and Pops would be, or should be, ready to go downstairs. This wedding was about to begin, as Lee had just announced.

"You look like a movie star, mom. And, Pops, you will look like the male lead in a 'beautiful wedding' segment on some US network if I can't sell this story to a Canadian network first. It's one hell of a story, mom, admit it."

"Hope, *language* dear. Not another cuss word on my wedding day, do you hear me?" Paradise realized she had snapped at her daughter, but maybe on her wedding day that was allowed.

Clearly it was okay with Hope. "Pops, let me pin your rose on your lapel," she said as she winked at her mother.

"Pin a rose on my what, young lady?" Pops was trying to lighten the moment and it worked.

At least it worked for him. His tears seem to have dried up, thank goodness. He couldn't imagine what people would think if he came down the stairs with these two beautiful young women and everyone saw him bawling like a baby.

"Mother, I didn't know you had bought wedding boots? I knew you were looking at a few different styles but clearly you went back and bought them. I love them so much. When you and dad get on the dance floor and everyone gets a teasing look at your boots you will immediately be the talk among the fashion leaders in the Cape. Will I be allowed to borrow them?"

"As long as your feet stop growing and you continue to wear the same size as me, of course you can borrow them."

As an afterthought Paradise added, "Not for a walk on the beach, though...high tide or low tide these are my 'show boots' and won't stand too much of a beating, understood? No steel toes included."

"Thanks for sharing, mom, and thanks for the continued beat down for wearing both my new blue party dress and my new rubber boots to the beach and then into the ocean years ago when I was a kid."

Laughing, Hope went on. "I know you're going to say memories are made of this, mom, and this is a good memory and I can laugh about it now, but in that moment I seemed to think I would get back at you if I ruined the most beautiful dress I ever owned...until now."

Hope twirled, and Pops caught her hand.

"Ladies, you are both my responsibility at the moment. Hope, you and I have to go downstairs and get your mother married. We have a full house, and, Paradise, I do mean a *full* house, and we are running late, so, assuming you two have nothing else that you absolutely have to talk about at this very moment let's—"

It seemed Hope wasn't through talking with her mother just yet."Sorry, Pops, and I'll be very quick. Mom, my wedding gift to you and daddy is the smooth running, no-mistakes-allowed wedding reception. I have almost an entire journal full of my timeline checks from the beginning to the end of the reception. You are not to worry about anything or anyone, got it?"

"Roger that, Hope. Roger that. Now let's get me married."

Paradise picked up her rose and handed one to Hope. "And do not make me laugh when I hand you my bouquet, which happens to be this rose."

Hope stepped out of the room and on to the first step of the stairs. "Pops, if you can keep two steps behind me, that gives me the chance to get out of the way at the bottom so our guests can feast their eyes on this beautiful bride."

One floor below, the instant Lee saw his mother he spread his arms and said to everyone, "Told ya.'"

"Mom, did you know your parents and dad's mother were all coming from Toronto? Look in the very back near the mudroom... they just came in." Hope wanted to bolt and hug her grandparents so much, but she would keep that thought close to her heart until the wedding ceremony was over.

"Hope, are you multi-tasking as we walk down the aisle?" Paradise saw her parents and gave them a big smile and a small wave. "I'm glad you saw them, sweetheart, but don't forget our vow to each other. 'Thou shall not multi-task until we are safely in front of Reverend Service.'"

"I guess I was!" Hope knew how happy this would make her parents. Family is everything and in the moment Hope felt it for perhaps the first time.

When she knew her mother was ready and the back of her dress was perfect, Hope made her way up the makeshift aisle. She was surprisingly nervous until Lee said, with great surprise, "Hope you look really pretty. You look like a girl!"

An audible gasp filled the room as Paradise came into full view on Pop's arm. Her floor-length wedding gown was spectacular in its simplicity. Very much the slip dress, as it was advertised from the front, but it was the back of her gown that even the men in the room seemed to appreciate.

The hemline in the back was longer and presented itself as a wanna-be train normally found as part of a veil. Hundreds of tiny hearts fought each other for space until they all gathered at the bottom of the dress. Not a heart to be seen on the front of her dress but the back was another story. The hearts appeared to have been sown on one at a time, but in fact they were part of the fabric of the dress.

"I heard them, my girl...all whispering about the back of your dress," Pops said. "Yes, the dress is pretty but you are absolutely beautiful, and with that I will give your hand to this kind man."

Pops turned to the groom. "Thomas, my job here is done so, if you will excuse me, I will find my bride."

Pops had done a bit of his own multi-tasking as the trio came down stairs and he knew exactly where to find Eugenie. He kissed Eugenie's hand then asked, "Did someone explain to you why I had been called upstairs? It seems like I was up there for a dozen hours before these two ladies were all primped and ready."

"Let's talk later, Pops. This part of our day will be over in a second so we should just pay attention. No chatter."

Well, okay then, Pops thought. But he did understand.

Turning to her daughter, Paradise passed her rose to Hope as they had discussed. Not wanting to make eye contact, she kept her eyes down as Hope reached in to hug her and whisper something in her ear. No one heard exactly what was said, but to the ladies in the front row it sounded like, "Do the deed, mother." Mother and daughter exchanged smiles and muffled chuckles.

Reverend Service was up next. After speaking softly to the bride and groom he spread his arms and said, "Let us pray." After a long minute, he lifted his head and asked everyone to take a seat if they could find one. "We are a full house here today."

Lee wanted to get *marriaged* right away so he could sit with his uncles, "And have some fun, too, sir. We re supposed to have fun."

"Hope and Lee have something to say to their parents on this special day. Hope, would you like to speak first?" Reverend Service said.

"No, I want to go first. Daddy, can I?"

"Absolutely," Thomas said.

There was a long and unexpected pause. Thomas and Hope leaned in, encouraging Lee to say what he had practised so hard by raising their eyebrows and tightening their stomach muscles. Suddenly, Lee was shy! "Can you say it for me, Hope?"

"What a novel idea." Hope, ever the comedian, drew laughter from everyone.

"My little brother and I are so happy you have asked us to be part of your special day. It is a dream come true to see our parents married...you'll have to wait for the movie to hear all the details. Lee and I stand with you today with immense love, and equal parts of pride and gratitude. We love you both so much. Congratulations, and enjoy your wedding day. Memories are made of this."

Turning to Lee, Hope added, "Little brother, we are now all *marriaged* so I think it's okay for you to go and find your uncles."

Running at full speed Lee shouted, "I already found them so I know where to go."

With that he jumped into Uncle Denis and Uncle Waine's arms. Denis gave a thumbs-up sign and the ceremony resumed.

Reverend Service surprised many when he announced that Paradise and Thomas had chosen to keep their vows private. "So, no need to lean in to see if you can hear what is being said, because that won't happen. Once the vows are exchanged, I will say a few prayers, the happy couple will sign the registry and I will present them to you. You'll be free to get up soon. I know many of you have been sitting for a rather long time."

The Reverend turned all of his attention to the lovely couple in front of him. When it was time for the vows, quiet murmurs could be heard first from Thomas and then from his bride.

"I think Paradise is crying. What do you think?" Pops was talking to his wife, who offered only a shrug of her shoulders. Pops might finally realize she's not kidding about being quiet. Eugenie could only hope.

Once the registry was signed, Hope gave her mom's rose back to her. There were hugs all around. Then Hope said "Remember now, you two, I am in charge of your reception. I have a list. Everything is taken care of and if I have missed anything I will address that when it happens. You are not to worry about anything. Got it?"

"Roger that."

"Roger that."

Reverent Service once again spread his arms wide. "Ladies and gentlemen will you please rise and welcome Lee, Hope, Paradise and Thomas Adams. Congratulations to all four of you."

Lee decided he shouldn't miss this so he ran, followed by the perfect slide right up to his sister's side. "Are we *marriaged* now? All of us?"

Picking his son up in his arms Thomas said, "My son, we are truly *marriaged* to each other. All four of us."

Turning to the throngs of people, some Thomas didn't think he had met, he said, "Welcome to our wedding reception, which, I believe has turned into a true Cape party! Please eat, drink and introduce yourself to someone you think is a stranger. By evening's end there will not be a stranger among us."

Hope jumped into action as everyone crowded around the bride and groom. "I'm going straight to our Toronto family and will let them know how welcome they are, how surprised and thrilled we are and that you will find your way to them, all in good time. So, you two have fun."

With that, Hope was off and running.

61: Best surprise ever!

Beryl Adams and Nancy and Ben Rhodes were relieved to see Hope seem to float around all other wedding guests to get to their side.

"Best surprise ever! Thank you so much for being with us to celebrate this long overdue marriage." Hope gathered all three in her embrace, and she managed to shed a tear on at least two of them. Not a tear among her grandparents.

"Is everything okay?" Hope asked as she dried her eyes. "You all seem sad or something."

Hope should have expected what came next from her Nana Adams. "This marriage should have taken place in a church. Only then will Paradise and my son be married in the eyes of our Lord."

Grandpa Rhodes jumped in. "Beryl, we talked about this. This is not the first thing we want to say to our beautiful granddaughter. But since you have said it, please don't repeat it again. Not to Paradise and Thomas, as we agreed on our long drive from the Halifax airport. Understood?"

"I understand. But this isn't right."

Grandma Rhodes realized her husband's words had not registered. "My dear friend, please don't make me regret asking you to come with Ben and me to see our children married. What has gotten into you? Don't answer that because you might have to admit that you weren't sincere when we talked about this, ending with your full agreement that you would not throw *your* beliefs at Paradise and Thomas. I'm disappointed in you, Beryl. And that's all I'll say here and now."

Turning to Hope, Nancy said, "My goodness, Hope, you are such a beautiful young lady. When you appeared on the staircase I wasn't sure it was you. Doesn't our granddaughter look wonderful,

Beryl?"

"Yes, you look good, Hope. I must say though, I'm surprised my son allowed you to wear such a revealing dress to his wedding, at your age."

Hope held her hands up to indicate her Grandma and Grandpa were not to speak up for her. "Nana, what is going on in that head of yours today? My mother and I bought our dresses together at the same store in Yarmouth and they were on sale. We both love what we're wearing, and isn't that the main thing today?"

Trying a different approach, Hope wrapped her arms around her Nana so no one else would hear what she added. "Nana, maybe you're not feeling well, so if you want I can take you to a room upstairs. I'll even fetch your luggage for you. But, so help me God, (I know, Bless me father for I have sinned….) please put your ugly away for today. Can you do that for me? Look at the size of my list. I'm in charge of the reception and if I have to worry about what you might say next, how am I going to leave your side?"

Beryl was ashamed of herself. "I owe all three of you an apology. And since we can't have a do-over, could you please forget what I have said since you joined us, Hope?"

"Done," Hope replied as she took off for her next assignment.

"And, done," Ben and Nancy said in unison.

"Hope, did you forget something?" Beryl was surprised to see her in front of them again.

"If any or all three of you would like to see Wilmot and Marie, please follow me. They are next on my list and they are in charge of food and drinks. Wait until you see the pile of food in our kitchen, in our mudroom and God knows where else. Okay that won't happen again Nana, and I apologize for speaking of God out of context." Hope led the way...

"Wilmot, just the man I'm looking for. Where is Marie?" Hope was in the kitchen doorway but her three surprise guests were not yet revealed. She was pretty sure Wilmot and Marie had been so consumed with their duties they would not have had a chance to even scan the crowd for a familiar face.

"I'm here, young lady, what can we do for you?" Marie said as she walked back into the kitchen from the very long food table now set up and oh-so-full of food.

"Genius idea, Hope, to have people approach the food from both sides of the table. But I'm not sure where all of these people are from. They can't all be from the Cape, can they?"

"I've been thinking about that," Wilmot said. He still had not seen his parents behind Hope. "And I do have an idea."

"Hold that thought, because I have three people very anxious to give you both a big hug."

Hope stepped aside and watched Wilmot and Marie reduced to tears when they saw the trio from Toronto.

"Marie," Hope said, looking at her list, "are you going to need some help? I see someone else brought Rapure yet it looks exactly like yours. What am I missing?" She was so impressed with how everything was set up for the exact time they had been given. Even the Rapure was hot, as it should be.

Wilmot had the answer. "As soon as the crowd grew I went back to our cottage to retrieve the Rapure that was meant for us. It seems we need both for today."

With the slightest nod between Nancy and Beryl the Toronto-two moved in to help Marie in any way they could. Within minutes they were trained, given their marching orders and ready to work.

Not to be outdone, Ben made his way around the women to get to Wilmot. "I hear you are in charge of all things liquid. I know my way around a good beer as well as a good bottle of wine or liquor. Can you use my help in any way? I'll work for free as long as you put a beer in my hand."

"Follow me," Wilmot said and just like that Hope had her backup plan for the kitchen.

Next up for Hope was to check in with Pops and Eugenie. She had a favour to ask. "Hi, you two. Do you have everything you need?"

Both nodded.

"I have a favour to ask. My plan was for Lee and I to spend the weekend elsewhere to give our parents privacy for at least a couple of days. But now with our Toronto grandparents arriving

I'm looking to find two bedrooms for them. If I could sleep on your sofa, and I'm pretty sure Lee can bunk in with his bachelor uncles, that frees up our bedrooms for out of town guests. If that's a problem, just say so, because I can also ask Mrs. Foss, who has invited me to sleep over many times when I babysit her twins."

Pops spoke first. "Hope, we would be delighted to have you stay with us for as many nights as you want."

Eugenie agreed, of course. "Hope, I will even make my famous French toast for your breakfast tomorrow, if you like. You will be in before breakfast, I hope"

"I will try to make it, but..." Then Hope was off and running to test her plan for Lee.

62: Beautiful stranger

Change of plans for Hope. She checked her work schedule against the time and realized she had an announcement to make. Buddy, the DJ she had personally interviewed for the gig, was all set up and had just given her the thumbs up, which she took to mean he was ready to start spinning records.

Passing the microphone to Hope, he mouthed, "It's live."

"Ladies and gentlemen, if I could have your attention for a minute or two...they tell me that you don't need a DJ at a Cape party because everyone arrives with whatever instrument they play. I'm not sure if that applies for wedding receptions, but I did see a couple of guitars in one of the bedrooms and a fiddle in another. I'm sure something can be worked out, so just come on up and talk with Buddy if you have a tune you want to play for my mom and dad."

Hope was of the opinion this should not happen, and she realized she shouldn't have sprung it on Buddy the way she did. She would speak with him when she passed the microphone back.

"And, of great importance at this very moment, please welcome our bride and groom to the dance floor for the first dance. Feel free to cut in, join in or watch the floor fill up from the comfort of your chair. I'll be back, but that's it for now. Buddy...back to you."

Denis and Waine had come forward with Lee and seemed to be waiting to speak with Hope. "Did one of you handsome men want to ask me to dance? Is that why you're here, Lee? Would you like to dance with me?"

Her brother looked at his uncles with a 'rescue me, please' look on his face. Then he stretched up toward Hope's ear and said, "Do you think mom and dad would let me sleep in #3 with my uncles tonight? If I can, and if I'm really good until the morning, they have a surprise for me. They won't tell me what it is, though."

"That's why it's called a surprise. Come with me to your room and bring your uncles. Meet you there in forty-five seconds."

Hope and Lee made it ahead of Denis and Waine, and Hope wondered if they both had bad knees. They sure didn't move fast. *Maybe they simply can't move quickly,* she thought.

When they appeared, somewhat out of breath, Hope gave them a cover. "Listen up. You had exactly the same idea as I did, Lee. If you could sleep at #3 while I'm sleeping at Pops and Eugenie's place, some of the overnight guests can have our rooms. So, pull out your jammies for a couple of nights and some clothes for the morning and we will pack everything in this backpack."

"Can we go right now?" Lee was very excited, but Hope wasn't sure Denis and Waine were ready to leave. She was about to ask what they wanted to do when Denis spoke.

"Waine needs his meds soon, and we're both tired, to be really honest, Hope, so if you could get us to the bride and groom so this little man can say goodnight we will be on our way. And, thanks for this. You're a great kid."

"Guess what, mom and dad, I'm moving out." Lee had raced to his parents.

"Is that right?" Thomas picked him up and gave him a long squeeze. "Do you have your own apartment?"

"No, silly, I'm moving in to #3 with my uncles."

Paradise said, "And who brought up the idea of this sleepover, Lee?"

Waine spoke up. "We asked Lee if he would like to come home with us, then Hope helped us pack his clothes and here we are hoping you will agree to our plan. And just sayin', Denis and I felt like we were being interrogated earlier today when it was just us and the local ladies before all these folks arrived. Denis, don't you think that's why we are bone-tired at this early hour?"

Hope was monitoring the lineup to talk with the guests of honour, so she stepped in. "I hate to break up this little family gathering, but the three of you get out of here and the two of you...back to your other guests."

Thinking she might need some interrogating skills of her own, Hope went in search of two hot-looking older guys who seemed to be making themselves right at home. She knew they had never stepped inside this house before. She was almost certain her parents didn't have a clue who they were.

Hope saw the two men under surveillance slip out the side door. *Oh no you don't,* she thought as she flew out the side door after them.

"Excuse me, do I know you gentlemen? Do you know my parents? Why are you here?"

"Which of those three questions would you like an answer first, Hope?"

"That doesn't fool me, I introduced myself at the microphone, so that's why you know my name. Were you even invited to this wedding?"

"I'm Clint and this is Jim Taylor. We are your parents' PI partners from Port Hope, Ontario. We were invited, but we kept our arrival a surprise. We came out this side door because we know exactly where your parents are at this very moment and we can slip out with them not having seen us. We thought we might go and check in to our hotel in Yarmouth. We were just talking about not coming back this evening, but perhaps arriving with breakfast in the morning. What do you think?"

Hope had to think on her feet to answer this one. She should have known Clint and Jim would attend. They were partners and friends with her mom and dad. Before Hope had properly met her mom there had been a shootout in Port Hope when her mom was there with Clint and Jim. It was her mom who took down the bad guy.

Hope wasn't sure she had all the details correct or in the right order but, in any case, *my mother is a bad-ass*, she thought, not for the first time.

"How about this. You arrive back here around 4 tomorrow afternoon rather than in the morning and bring three large pizzas with you. I will only tell mom and dad that I have ordered pizza to be delivered, so your secret is safe with me. I hope it will be only our immediate family, but, as you have seen by the number of locals here, I can't make any promises."

"Perfect, and this is our car rental right here, so let us get out of your way. It's clear you are in charge, Hope, so back at it, girl."

Too late, Hope wondered if Clint and Jim had seen her parents shingle hung out in their honour. 'PIU – the Cape Crew.' *They are two lovely looking men, no question about that.*

Hope saw Reverend Service coming out the same side door. Fortunately she had a gift from her parents for the Reverend in her folder and glued to her hip. She approached Reverend Service, thanked him again, gave him the envelope she had been trusted to deliver and helped him navigate getting out after, as his car was wedged in between a couple of late-arriving trucks.

Tapping on his car window to indicate he was clear to drive forward and away, Hope couldn't help herself. "Reverend Service, if this Reverend thing doesn't work out for you, I can vouch for you to be a driving instructor at local schools."

She could hear his laughter as he drove off.

Hope liked Reverend Service and made a mental note to ask her parents which church was his. She might like to attend service there one day. Not tomorrow, though.

Next stop was back to the DJ, who might be wrapping up any time now. How had it gotten so late?

She was surprised to see the crowd had thinned out considerably in the last hour. Hope had the DJ's money in her folder, too, and she reminded him to give her the heads up by playing *Old Time Rock n Roll* just before he announced the last dance of the evening.

Hope knew they had another half hour of dancing, but she wanted to talk with her parents about how she planned to wrap this up and get everyone out of their home by midnight. They actually found her and were both gushing about how organized she was and how smoothly everything had gone.

Hope didn't want to jinx it because everything was leading up to the last dance. That had to be perfect. "In about twenty minutes

Buddy will invite any remaining guests to join you both on the dance floor for the last dance. And..."

Clearly something or someone had caught Hope's eye. "Oh. My. God. Sorry mother but I'm looking at a guy who has been here all evening. He is totally hot and so lovely and everyone but me seems to know him. I haven't seen him on the dance floor, but I am going to change that. Right now."

Thomas was suddenly on full alert. *Him*? Who is *him*, Hope?"

"That's exactly what I am about to find out."

Hope knew the lovely stranger was watching her as she zoned in on his face and walked the length of the dance floor to introduce herself.

"Hi. I'm Hope." She extended her hand only to have this hottie lift her hand to his mouth so he could kiss it.

"Oh, girl, I know who you are. I have been watching you all evening. Do you have any idea how beautiful you are right this minute? And don't even get me started on your dress."

"Not you, too. You don't think it looks like I'm wearing a slip, do you?"

"I'm trying very hard to not go there at the moment."

The beautiful stranger was laughing as he slipped his arm around her. "Hope, may I have this dance?"

"Not until you tell me your name."

"Sorry, I'm Ben, and I'm thrilled to meet you."

Buddy announced the next song would be *Old Time Rock n Roll*.

"Still want to dance with me?" Hope was smiling as they stepped on to the dance floor.

Twirling her around and around Ben leaned down so he could be heard over the music, "I need the next dance, too."

"Roger that," Hope replied.

Buddy announced that the next dance would be the last one and invited everyone to join the bride and groom.

"This is my parents' favourite song," Hope said to Ben as *Save The Last Dance With Me* filled the speakers.

"Hope, I love this song. Maybe one day this will be our song, too," he whispered in her ear as they joined her parents on the dance floor.

Memories are made of this.

Carol Ann Cole

Acknowledgements

I want to profoundly thank everyone who continues to express interest in the *Paradise Series. You* are the reason I continue to write, and your support means the world to me. Keep your comments coming!

Connie Dea, thank you, dear, for all that you do to help me during my writing process. Up next for us, *the Cole Connection*!

Brenda Thompson, owner and publisher at Moose House Publications, thank you for your support and guidance. I take a great deal of pride in being one of your growing number of authors.

Andrew Wetmore, my editor, I continue to learn from you, and appreciate all that you have given me...my writer's tool kit is overflowing.

Carol Ann Cole

About the author

Carol Ann Cole is a best-selling author with four non-fiction books and four novels to her credit.

Currently she is writing two very different books. *The Cole Connection* is non-fiction to be published in November 2022, and the fifth instalment in *the Paradise Series* will be released in mid-2023.

Additionally, Carol Ann is one of twenty-plus authors, all with Moose House Publications, who are *collectively* writing a novel, *Less Than Innocent*, due out in the fall of 2022.

Carol Ann calls Halifax 'home' but family and friends draw her to Toronto as well.

CPSIA information can be obtained
at www.ICGtesting.com
Printed in the USA
BVHW051407130522
636973BV00017B/417

9 781990 187285